DOVER · THRIFT · EDITIONS

Five Great
Short Stories

ANTON CHEKHOV

DOVER PUBLICATIONS, INC.
New York

ANTON PAVLOVICH CHEKHOV (1860–1904): Russian physician and preeminent author of short stories and plays. The present volume contains five of his most highly regarded stories, set in a variety of Tsarist Russian milieux and representative of the basic themes of his oeuvre: the sociological and psychological obstacles in the way of human affection and satisfactory development of the personality.

Contents

DOVER THRIFT EDITIONS

EDITOR: STANLEY APPELBAUM

Published in Canada by General Publishing Company, Ltd., 30 Lesmill Road, Don Mills, Toronto, Ontario.
Published in the United Kingdom by Constable and Company, Ltd.

This Dover edition, first published in 1990, is an unabridged republication of five stories. "The Black Monk" and "The Peasants" are reprinted from *The Works of Anton Chekhov: One Volume Edition*, Black's Readers Service Company, N.Y., n.d. (ca. 1929; translators not credited). "The House with the Mezzanine," "Gooseberries" and "The Lady with the Toy Dog" are reprinted from *My Life and Other Stories*, C. W. Daniel, Ltd., London, 1920 (translated by S. S. Koteliansky and Gilbert Cannan). A number of typographical errors have been corrected tacitly. Footnotes glossing Russian terms remaining in the translated texts have been prepared specially for this Dover edition.

Manufactured in the United States of America
Dover Publications, Inc., 31 East 2nd Street, Mineola, N.Y. 11501

Library of Congress Cataloging-in-Publication Data

Chekhov, Anton Pavlovich, 1860–1904.
[Short stories. English. Selections]
Five great short stories / Anton Chekhov.
p.   cm. — (Dover thrift editions)
Translated from the Russian.
Contents: The black monk — The house with the mezzanine — The peasants — Gooseberries — The lady with the toy dog.
ISBN 0-486-26463-7 (pbk.)
1. Chekhov, Anton Pavlovich, 1860–1904—Translations, English.
I. Title. II. Series.
PG3456.A13   1990
891.73'3—dc20   90-3580
                                    CIP

The Black Monk

CHAPTER I

Nerves

ANDREY VASIL'ICH KOVRIN, Master of Arts, was overworked and
nervous. He was not being treated, but one day while sitting with a
doctor at wine he happened casually to speak about his health. The
physician advised him to pass the spring and summer in the country.
Opportunely he received then a long letter from Tania Pesotski,
inviting him to visit Borisovka. He decided that he really required a
change.

It was April. He went to his family estate of Kovrinka for three
weeks; then, the roads being clear, he started on wheels to see his
former guardian and tutor, Pesotski, the great horticulturist. From
Kovrinka to Borisovka, where the Pesotskis lived, it was only seventy
versts,* and it was a pleasure to take the drive.

Egor Semenych Pesotski's house was huge, with columns and lions,
but the plaster was cracking. The old park, severe and gloomy, laid out
in the English style, extended for nearly a verst from the house to the
river, and finished in abruptly precipitous clayey banks, on which there
grew old pines with bare roots that looked like shaggy paws; down below
the water glittered unsociably, and snipe flitted along its surface with
plaintive cries. When there you always had the feeling that you must sit
down and write a ballad. However, near the house, in the courtyard and
in the fruit orchard, which together with the nurseries covered about
thirty acres, it was gay and cheerful even in bad weather. Such
wonderful roses, lilies and camellias, such tulips of all imaginable hues,
beginning with brilliant white and finishing with tints as black as soot,
such a wealth of flowers as Pesotski possessed Kovrin had never seen in
any other place. It was only the beginning of spring, and the real
luxuriance of the flower-beds was still hidden in the hot-houses; but

*[*Verstá*, slightly over a kilometer; about ⅔ of a mile.]

1

even those which blossomed in the borders along the walks and here and there on the flower-beds were sufficient to make you feel, when you passed through the garden, that you were in the kingdom of delicate tints, especially in the early morning, when a dewdrop glistened brightly on each petal.

The decorative part of the garden, which Pesotski called contemptuously a mere trifle, had greatly impressed Kovrin in his childhood. What wonderful whimsicalities were to be found there, what far-fetched monstrosities and mockeries of nature! There were espaliers of fruit trees, pear trees that had the form of pyramidal poplars, oaks and limes shaped like balls, an umbrella made of an apple tree, arches, monograms, candelabra and even 1862 formed by a plum tree; this date denoted the year when Pesotski first began to occupy himself with horticulture. There you also found pretty, graceful trees with straight strong stems like palms, and only when you examined them closely you saw that they were gooseberries and currants. But what chiefly made the garden pay and produced an animated appearance was the constant movement in it. From early morning till evening people with wheelbarrows, shovels and watering-pots swarmed like ants round the trees, bushes, avenues and flower-beds.

Kovrin arrived at the Pesotskis' in the evening, at past nine o'clock. He found Tania and her father in a very anxious mood. The clear starlit sky and the falling thermometer foretold a morning frost; the head gardener, Ivan Karlych, had gone to town, and there was nobody who could be relied on. During supper nothing but morning frost was talked of, and they settled that Tania was not to go to bed, but walk through the gardens and see if all was in order after midnight, and that her father would get up at three or probably earlier.

Kovrin sat up with Tania, and after midnight he went with her into the orchard. It was very cold. In the yard there was a strong smell of burning. In the large orchard, which was called the commercial orchard and brought Egor Semenych a clear yearly profit of several thousand roubles, a thick, black, biting smoke spread along the earth, and by enveloping the trees saved those thousands from the frost. The trees were planted here in regular rows like the squares of a chess-board, and they looked like ranks of soldiers. This strictly pedantical regularity together with the exact size and similarity of the stems and crowns of the trees made the picture monotonous and dull. Kovrin and Tania passed along the rows, where bonfires of manure, straw and all sorts of refuse were smouldering, and occasionally they met workmen, who were wandering about in the smoke like shadows. Only plums, cherries and some sorts of apple trees were in full blossom, but the whole orchard was smothered in smoke, and it was only when they reached the nurseries that Kovrin could draw a long breath.

"From my childhood the smoke here has made me sneeze," he said, shrugging his shoulders; "but I still do not understand how this smoke can protect the trees from frost."

"The smoke takes the place of clouds, when they are absent . . ." Tania answered.

"Why are clouds necessary?"

"In dull and cloudy weather there is never night frost."

"Really?"

He laughed and took her hand. Her broad, serious, cold face, with its finely marked black eyebrows, the high turned-up collar of her coat, which prevented her from moving her head with ease, her whole thin, *svelte* figure, with skirts well tucked up to protect them from the dew, affected him.

"Good Lord, she's already grown up!" he said. "When I last drove away from here, five years ago, you were still quite a child. You were a thin, long-legged, bare-headed girl in short petticoats, and I teased you and called you the heron. . . . What time does!"

"Yes, five years!" Tania sighed. "Much water has flowed away since then. Tell me, Andryusha, quite candidly," she said rapidly, looking into his face, "have we become strangers to you? But, why should I ask? You're a man, you are now living your own interesting life, you are great. . . . Estrangement is so natural! But, however it may be, Andryusha, I want you to consider us as your own people. We have that right."

"Of course you have, Tania!"

"Honour bright?"

"Yes, honour bright."

"You were surprised to-day to see we had so many of your portraits. You know my father adores you. Sometimes I think that he loves you more than he does me. He is proud of you. You are a scholar, an extraordinary man, you have made a brilliant career, and he is convinced that you have become all that because he brought you up. I do not prevent him from thinking this. Let him."

The day began to break; this was chiefly to be noticed by the distinctness with which the clouds of smoke were perceptible in the air, and the bark of the trees became visible. Nightingales were singing and the cry of the quail was borne from the fields.

"It's time to go to bed now," Tania said. "How cold it is!" She took his arm. "Thank you, Andryusha, for coming. We have but few acquaintances here, and they are not interesting. We have nothing but the garden, the garden, the garden—nothing but that. Standard, half-standard," she laughed. "pippins, rennets, codlins, grafting, budding. . . . All, all our life has gone into the garden—I never dream of anything but apples and pears. Of course, all this is good and useful, but sometimes I wish for something else for variety. I remember when you used to come for the holidays or simply on a visit the house seemed to grow fresher and lighter; it was as if the covers had been taken off the lustres and the chairs. I was a child then, still I understood."

She talked for a long time and with great feeling. Suddenly the idea entered his head that in the course of the summer he might become attached to this little, weak, loquacious creature, he might be carried away and fall in love—in their position it was so possible and so natural! This thought amused and moved him; he bent over her charming troubled face and began to sing in a low voice:

"Onegin, I'll not hide from you
I love Tatiana madly . . ."

When they reached the house, Egor Semenych was already up. Kovrin did not want to sleep; he began to talk with the old man and he returned with him to the garden. Egor Semenych was a tall, broad-shouldered man with a large stomach; he suffered from breathlessness, but he always walked so fast that it was difficult to keep up with him. He always had an extremely worried look, and he was always hurrying somewhere, with an expression that seemed to say if he were too late by one minute even, all would be lost!

"Here's a strange thing, my dear fellow," he said, stopping to take breath. "It's freezing on the ground, as you see, but if you raise the thermometer on a stick about fourteen feet above earth it's warm there. . . . Why is it?"

"I really don't know," Kovrin said, laughing.

"Hm. . . . Of course, one can't know everything. . . . However vast a man's understanding may be it can't comprehend everything. You've chiefly gone in for philosophy?"

"Yes. I lecture on psychology, but I study philosophy in general."

"And it does not bore you?"

"On the contrary, it's my very existence."

"Well, may God prosper your work . . ." Egor Semenych exclaimed, and he stroked his grey whiskers reflectively. "God prosper you! . . . I'm very glad for you. . . . Very glad, indeed, my boy. . . ."

Suddenly he seemed to listen, an expression of anger passed over his face and he ran off to one side and was soon lost to sight among the trees in the clouds of smoke.

"Who has tethered a horse to an apple tree?" his despairing, heartrending cry could be heard. "What villain and scoundrel has dared to tie a horse to an apple-tree? Good God, good God! They have dirtied, spoilt, damaged, ruined it. The orchard is lost! The orchard is destroyed! My God!"

When he returned to Kovrin he looked worn out and insulted.

"What can you do with this accursed people?" he said in a plaintive voice, clasping his hands. "Stepka was carting manure during the night and has tied his horse to an apple tree! The villain tied the reins so tight round it that the bark has been rubbed in three places. What do you think of that! I spoke to him, and he only stood open-mouthed, blinking his eyes! He ought to be hanged."

When he was somewhat calmer he embraced Kovrin and kissed him on the cheek.

"Well, God help you. . . . God help you . . ." he mumbled. "I'm very glad you've come. Delighted beyond words. . . . Thank you."

Then he went round the whole garden at the same rapid pace and with the same troubled expression, and showed his former ward all the hot-houses, conservatories and fruit-sheds, also his two apiaries, which he called the wonder of the century.

While they were walking round the sun rose and shed its brilliant rays over the garden. It became warm. Foreseeing a bright, joyous and long day, Kovrin remembered it was only the beginning of May, and that the whole summer lay before them, also bright, joyous and long, and suddenly a gladsome, youthful feeling was aroused in his breast, like he used to have when running about that garden in his childhood. He embraced the old man and kissed him tenderly. They were both much affected as they went into the house, where they drank tea with cream out of old china cups, and ate rich satisfying cracknels—these trifles again reminded Kovrin of his childhood and youth. The beautiful present and the memories that were aroused in him of the past were blended together; his soul was full and rejoiced.

He waited for Tania to get up and had coffee with her and then a walk, after which he went into his own room and sat down to work. He read with attention, made notes, only raising his eyes from time to time to look out of the open window, or at the fresh flowers, still wet with dew that were in a vase on his table, and then he again lowered his eyes to his book, and it appeared to him that every nerve in his system vibrated with satisfaction.

CHAPTER II

A Pale Face!

IN THE COUNTRY he continued to lead the same nervous and restless life as in town. He read and wrote very much, he learned Italian, and when he was walking he thought all the time of the pleasure he would have in sitting down to work again. Everybody was astonished how little he slept; if he happened to doze for half an hour during the day he would afterwards not sleep all night, and after a sleepless night he felt himself active and gay, as if nothing had happened.

He talked much, drank wine and smoked expensive cigars. Often, indeed almost every day, some young girls from a neighbouring estate, friends of Tania's, came to the Pesotskis'. They played on the piano and sang together. Sometimes another neighbour, a young man, who played the violin very well, came too. Kovrin listened to the music and singing with avidity, and he was quite overcome by it, which was evidenced by his eyes closing and his head sinking on one side.

One day after the evening tea he was sitting on the balcony reading. At that time Tania (a soprano), one of her friends (a contralto) and the young man playing on his violin were practicing Braga's celebrated serenade. Kovrin tried to make out the words—they were Russian— and he was quite unable to understand their meaning. At last laying his book aside and listening attentively he understood: A girl with a diseased imagination heard one night mysterious sounds in the garden, which were so wonderfully beautiful and strange that she thought they were holy harmonies, but so incomprehensible for us mortals that they ascended again to heaven. Once more Kovrin's eyes began to close. He rose, and feeling quite exhausted he began to walk about the drawing- room and then about the dancing hall. When they stopped singing he took Tania's arm and led her on to the balcony.

"Ever since the morning an old legend has been running in my head," he said. "I don't remember if I read it, or whether it was told me, but the legend is a strange one, and not like any other. To begin with it is not very clear. A thousand years ago a certain monk, clad in black, was walking in the desert somewhere in Syria or Arabia. . . . A few miles from the place where he was walking some fishermen saw another black monk moving slowly across the surface of a lake. This other monk was a mirage. Now you must forget all the laws of optics, which the legend evidently does not admit, and listen to the continuation. From the mirage another mirage was obtained, and from that one a third, so that the image of the black monk was reproduced without end in one sphere of the atmosphere after another. He was seen sometimes in Africa, sometimes in Spain, sometimes in India, then again in the far North. ... At last he went beyond the bounds of the earth's atmosphere and is now wandering over the whole universe, always unable to enter into the conditions where he would be able to disappear. Perhaps at present he may be seen somewhere on Mars or on some star of the Southern Cross. But, my dear, the main point, the very essence of the whole legend, consists in this, that exactly a thousand years from the time the monk was walking in the desert the mirage will again be present in the atmosphere of the world, and it will show itself to men. It appears that those thousand years are nearly accomplished. .... Accordingly to the legend we can expect the Black Monk either to-day or to-morrow."

"A strange mirage," Tania said. She did not like the legend.

"But the strangest thing is that I can't remember from where this legend has got into my head," Kovrin said, laughing. "Have I read it? Was it told me? Or perhaps I have dreamed about the Black Monk? By God, I can't remember. But the legend interests me. I think of it all day long."

Allowing Tania to return to her guests he left the house, and plunged in meditation he passed along the flower-beds. The sun was already setting. The flowers, perhaps because they had just been watered, exhaled a moist irritating odour. In the house they had again begun to sing, and at that distance the fiddle sounded like a human voice. Kovrin, straining his memory to remember where he had heard or read the legend, bent his steps towards the park, walking slowly, and imperceptibly he arrived at the river.

Running down the steep footpath that passed by the bare roots he came to the water, disturbing some snipe and frightening a pair of ducks. Some of the tops of the gloomy pines were still illuminated by the rays of the setting sun, but on the surface of the river evening had already settled down. Kovrin crossed the footbridge to the other bank. Before him lay a wide field of young rye not yet in flower. Neither a human habitation nor a living soul was to be seen near or far, and it seemed as if this footpath, if only you went far enough along it, would lead to that unknown, mysterious place into which the sun had just descended, and where the glorious blaze of the evening brightness was still widespread.

"What space, what freedom, what quiet is here!" Kovrin thought as he went along the footpath. "It seems as if the whole world was looking at me dissembling and waiting, that I should understand it. . . ."

But just then waves passed over the rye and a light wind touched his bare head. A minute later there was again a gust of wind, but a stronger one. The rye began to rustle, and behind it the dull murmur of the pines was heard. Kovrin stopped in amazement. On the horizon something like a whirlwind or a water-spout—a high black column, stretched from the earth to the sky. Its outlines were indistinct; from the first minute it was evident that it did not remain on one spot, but was moving with terrible rapidity—moving straight towards Kovrin, and the nearer it came the smaller and clearer it became. Kovrin rushed to one side into the rye to make room for it, and he had scarcely time to do so. . . .

A monk clad in black, with a grey head and black eyebrows, his arms crossed on his breast, was borne past him. . . . His bare feet did not touch the earth. He had already passed Kovrin for a distance of about twelve feet, when he looked back at him, nodded his head and smiled affably, but at the same time cunningly. What a pale—a terribly pale—and thin face! Again beginning to grow larger, he flew across the river, struck noiselessly against the clayey bank and the pines and, passing through them, disappeared like smoke.

"Well, you see?" Kovrin mumbled. "So the legend is true."

Without trying to explain to himself this strange apparition, but feeling pleased that he had chanced to be so close, and had seen so distinctly not only the black garb, but even the monk's face and eyes, he returned home in pleasant agitation.

In the park and the gardens people were quietly moving about; in the house they were playing—that meant he alone had seen the monk. He was very anxious to tell Tania and Egor Semenych all he had seen, but he thought that they would certainly consider his words mere nonsense, and it would frighten them—it was best to remain silent. He laughed loudly, he sang and danced the mazurka, he was gay and everybody—the guests and Tania—thought that his face had never looked so radiant and inspired, and that he certainly was a most interesting man.

CHAPTER III

She Loves

AFTER SUPPER, when their guests had departed, he went to his room and lay down on the sofa: he wanted to think about the monk. But a minute later Tania entered the room.

"Here, Andryusha, are some of father's articles; read them," she said, giving him a parcel of pamphlets and proofs. "They are splendid articles. He writes very well."

"Well, indeed," said Egor Semenych, with a forced laugh, following her into the room; he was confused. "Don't listen to her, please, and don't read them. However, if you want to go to sleep you may as well read them: they are excellent soporifics."

"I think them excellent articles," Tania said, with deep conviction. "Read them, Andryusha, and persuade papa to write oftener. He might write a whole course of horticulture."

Egor Semenych forced a laugh, blushed and began to say such phrases as confused authors are wont to say. At last he gave in.

"If you must, then first read this article by Gaucher and these Russian notices," he murmured, turning the pamphlets over with trembling hands, "or else you won't understand it. Before reading my refutation you must know what I refute. However, it's all non-sense . . . and very dull. Besides, I should say it's time to go to bed."

Tania left the room. Egor Semenych sat down on the sofa next to Kovrin and sighed deeply.

"Yes, my dear fellow . . ." he began after a short silence. "So it is, my most amiable Master of Arts. Here am I writing articles, taking part in exhibitions, receiving medals. . . . People say Pesotski has apples the size of a man's head, people say Pesotski has made a fortune by his orchards and gardens. In a word, 'Kochubey is rich and famous.' Query: To what does all this lead? The garden is really beautiful—a model garden. . . . It is not simply a garden, it is an institution, possessing great importance for the empire, because it is, so to speak, a step in a new era of Russian economy—of Russian industry. But what for? For what object?"

"The business speaks for itself."

"That is not what I mean. I ask: What will become of the gardens when I die? In the condition you see it now, it will not exist for a single month without me. The whole secret of its success is not because the garden is large and there are many labourers, but because I love the work—you understand? I love it, perhaps more than my own self. Look at me. I do everything myself. I work from morning to night. I do all the grafting myself. I do all the pruning myself—all the planting— everything. When I am assisted I am jealous and irritable to rudeness. The whole secret lies in love, that is, in the vigilant master's eye, in the master's hand too, in the feeling that when you go anywhere, to pay a visit of an hour, you sit there and your heart is not easy; you're not quite yourself, you're afraid something may happen in the garden.

When I die who will look after it all? Who will work? A gardener?
Workmen? Yes? I tell you, my good friend, the chief enemy in our
business is not the hare, not the cockchafer, not the frost, but the
stranger."

"But Tania?" Kovrin asked, laughing. "She can't be more injurious
than the hare. She loves and understands the business."

"Yes, she loves and understands it. If after my death she gets the
garden, and becomes the mistress, I could wish for nothing better. But
if, God forbid it, she should get married?" Egor Semenych whispered
and looked at Kovrin with alarm. "That's just what I fear! She gets
married, children arrive, and then there's no time to think of the
garden. What I chiefly fear is that she'll get married to some young
fellow, who'll be stingy and will let the garden to some tradesman, and
the whole place will go to the devil in the first year! In our business
women are the scourge of God!"

Egor Semenych sighed and was silent for a few moments.

"Perhaps it is egoism, but, to speak frankly, I don't want Tania to
marry. I'm afraid. There's a young fop with a fiddle, who comes here
and scrapes at it; I know very well Tania will not marry him. I know it
very well, but I can't bear him! In general, dear boy, I'm a great oddity.
I confess it."

Egor Semenych rose and paced about the room for some time, much
agitated; it was evident that he wanted to say something very
important, but could not make up his mind to do so.

"I love you very much, and will speak to you quite frankly," he said
at last, and thrust his hands into his pockets. "There are certain ticklish
subjects I regard quite simply, and I say quite openly what I think of
them. I cannot bear so-called hidden thoughts. I say to you plainly: You
are the only man I would not be afraid to give my daughter to. You are a
clever man, you have a good heart, and you would not allow my
cherished work to perish. But the chief reason is—I love you as if you
were my son—and I am proud of you. If you and Tania could settle a
little romance between yourselves, why—what then? I would be very
glad—very happy! As an honest man I say this quite openly, without
mincing matters."

Kovrin laughed. Egor Semenych opened the door to leave the room,
but he stopped on the threshold.

"If a son were to be born to you and Tania I'd make a gardener of
him," he said reflectively. "However, these are empty thoughts. . . .
Sleep well!"

Left alone, Kovrin lay down more comfortably on the sofa and began
to look through the articles. One was entitled: "Of Intermediate
Culture," another was called: "A few words concerning Mr. Z——'s

remarks on the digging up of ground for a new garden," a third was: "More about the budding of dormant eyes"; they were all of a similar nature. But what an uneasy, uneven tone, what nervous, almost unhealthy passion! Here was an article one would suppose of the most peaceful nature, and on the most indifferent subject: it was about the Russian Antonov apple. However, Egor Semenych began with, "*audiatur altera pars*," and finished, "*sapienti sat*," and between these two quotations there was quite a fountain of various poisonous words addressed to the "learned ignorance of our qualified gardeners who observe nature from the height of their cathedras," or else M. Gaucher, "whose success has been created by the unlearned and the dilettante." Here again, quite out of place, was an insincere regret that it was now no longer possible to flog the peasants who stole fruit and broke the trees.

"The work is pretty, charming, healthy, but even here are passions and war," Kovrin thought. "It must be that everywhere and in all arenas of human activity intellectual people are nervous and remarkable for their heightened sensitiveness. Apparently this is necessary."

He thought of Tania, who was so delighted with her father's articles. She was small, pale and so thin that her collar-bones were visible; she had dark, wide-open clever eyes that were always looking into something, searching for something; her gait was short-stepped and hurried like her father's; she spoke much, she liked to argue, and then even the most unimportant phrase was accompanied by expressive looks and gestures. She certainly was nervous to the highest degree.

Kovrin continued to read, but he could understand nothing, so he threw the book away. The same pleasant excitement he had felt when he danced the mazurka and listened to the music now overcame him again, and aroused in him numberless thoughts. He rose and began to walk about the room, thinking of the black monk. It entered his head that if he alone had seen this strange supernatural monk it must be because he was ill and had hallucinations. This reflection alarmed him, but not for long.

"But I feel very well, and I do nobody any harm; therefore there is nothing bad in my hallucinations," he thought, and he again felt quite contented.

He sat down on the sofa and seized his head in both hands, trying to restrain the incomprehensible joy that filled his whole being, then he went to the table and began to work. But the thoughts he read in the books did not satisfy him. He wanted something gigantic, immense, astounding. Towards morning he undressed and reluctantly lay down in bed: he ought to sleep!

When he heard Egor Semenych's footsteps going down to the

garden, Kovrin rang the bell and ordered the man-servant to bring him some wine. He drank several glasses of Château-Lafite with pleasure, and then covered himself up to the head; his senses became dim and he went to sleep.

CHAPTER IV

Tears of Tania

EGOR SEMENYCH and Tania often quarreled and said unpleasant things to each other.

One morning they had a quarrel. Tania began to cry and went to her room. She did not appear at dinner nor at tea. At first Egor Semenych went about looking very important and sulky, as if he wished everybody to know that for him the interests of justice and order stood above everything in the world, but soon he was unable to maintain that character and became depressed. He wandered sadly about the park and constantly sighed: "Oh, good God, good God!" At dinner he would not eat a crumb. At last feeling guilty and having qualms of conscience he knocked at his daughter's locked door and called to her timidly:

"Tania, Tania!"

And in answer he heard on the other side of the door a weak voice exhausted with crying, but still very positive, reply:

"Leave me alone, I beg you!"

The master's trouble affected the whole house, even the people working in the garden were under its influence. Kovrin was immersed in his own interesting work, but at last he too became sad and felt awkward. In order in some measure to dissipate the general gloomy mood he decided to intervene, and early in the evening he knocked at Tania's door. He was admitted.

"Oh, oh, what a shame!" he began jokingly, looking with astonishment at Tania's tear-stained, sad little face that was all covered with red blotches. "Is it possible it is so serious? Oh, oh!"

"If you only knew how he tortures me!" she said, and tears—bitter, plentiful tears—welled up in her large eyes. "He has worn me quite out!" she continued, wringing her hands. "I said nothing to him . . . nothing at all. . . . I only said there is no need to keep . . . extra workmen if . . . if it is possible to get day labourers whenever they are wanted. Why, why the workmen have been doing nothing for a whole week. . . . I . . . I only said this and he shouted at me and he told me . . . many offensive, many deeply insulting things. Why, why?"

"Enough! Enough!" Kovrin said as he arranged a lock of her hair. "You have abused each other, you have wept, and that's enough. One must not be angry for long, that's wrong . . . all the more because he loves you tenderly."

"He . . . he has spoilt my whole life," Tania continued. "I am only insulted and . . . wounded here. He considers me superfluous in his house. What am I to do? He is right. I'll go away from here to-morrow and become a telegraph girl. . . . Let him . . ."

"Well, well, well. . . . Tania, don't cry. You mustn't, my dear. . . . You are both hot-headed, irritable, and you are both in fault. Come along, I'll make peace between you."

Kovrin spoke affectionately and persuasively, but she continued to cry, her shoulders shaking and her hands clenched, as if a terrible misfortune had befallen her. He was all the more sorry for her because her grief was not serious, yet she suffered deeply. What trifles were sufficient to make this poor creature unhappy for a whole day, yes, perhaps even for her whole life! While comforting Tania, Kovrin thought that besides this girl and her father he might search the whole world without being able to find any other people who loved him as one of their family. If it had not been for these two people perhaps he, who had lost both his parents in his early childhood, would not have known to his very death what sincere affection was, nor that naïve, uncritical love that only exists between very near blood relatives. And he felt that his half-diseased, overtaxed nerves were drawn towards the nerves of this weeping, shuddering girl as iron is drawn to the magnet. He could never love a healthy, strong, red-cheeked woman, but pale, fragile, unhappy Tania attracted him.

He was pleased to stroke her hair, pat her shoulders, press her hands and wipe away her tears. At last she stopped crying; but for a long time she continued to complain about her father, and of her difficult, unbearable life in that house, begging Kovrin to enter into her position; then she gradually began to smile and to sigh that God had given her such a bad character, and at last she laughed aloud, called herself a fool and ran out of the room.

Shortly after, when Kovrin went into the garden, Egor Semenych and Tania were walking together in the avenue eating black bread and salt (they were both hungry), as if nothing had happened.

CHAPTER V

Red Spots

DELIGHTED THAT the part of peacemaker had been successful, Kovrin went into the park. While sitting on a bench thinking he heard the sound of wheels and of girls' laughter—visitors had arrived. When the shades of evening had begun to settle down on the gardens faint sounds of a violin and of voices singing reached his ear, and this reminded him of the black monk. Where, in what land or on what planet was that optical incongruity now being borne?

He had scarcely remembered the legend, and recalled to his memory the dark vision he had seen in the rye field, when just before him a middle-sized man with a bare grey head and bare feet, who looked like a beggar, came silently out of the pine wood, walking with small, unheard steps. On his pale, deathlike face the black eyebrows stood out sharply. Nodding affably this beggar or pilgrim came noiselessly and sat down on the bench. Kovrin recognized in him the black monk. For a minute they looked at each other—Kovrin with astonishment; the monk in a kindly and, as on the previous occasion, in a somewhat cunning manner, and with a self-complacent expression.

"But you are a mirage," Kovrin exclaimed; "why are you here and sitting in one place too? That is not in accordance with the legend."

"That's all the same," the monk replied after a pause, in a low quiet voice, turning his face towards Kovrin. "The mirage, the legend and I are all the products of your excited imagination. I am a phantom."

"Then, you do not exist?" Kovrin asked.

"Think what you like," the monk answered with a faint smile. "I exist in your imagination, and your imagination is part of nature, consequently I exist in nature too."

"You have a very old, clever and expressive face; just as if you had really existed for more than a thousand years," Kovrin said. "I did not know that my imagination was capable of creating such phenomena. But why are you looking at me with such rapture? Do I please you?"

"Yes. You are one of the few who are justly called the chosen of God. You serve the eternal truth. Your thoughts, your intentions, your extraordinary science and your whole life bear the godlike, the heavenly stamp, as they are devoted to the reasonable and the beautiful, that is to say, to that which is eternal."

"You said the eternal truth. . . . But can people attain to the eternal truth, and is it necessary for them if there is no eternal life?"

"There is eternal life," the monk answered.

"Do you believe in the immortality of man?"

"Yes, of course. A great brilliant future awaits you men. And the more men like you there are on earth, the sooner this future will be realized. Without you, the servants of the first cause, you who live with discernment and in freedom, the human race would, indeed, be insignificant. Developing in a natural way it would long have waited for the end of its earthly history. You are leading it to the kingdom of eternal truth several thousand years sooner—and in this lies your great service. . . . You incarnate in yourselves the blessing with which God has honoured mankind."

"But what is the object of eternal life?" Kovrin asked.

"The same as of all life—enjoyment. True enjoyment is knowledge, and eternal life offers numberless and inexhaustible sources of knowledge; this is the meaning of: 'in my Father's House are many mansions.'"

"If you only knew how pleasant it is to listen to you," Kovrin said, rubbing his hands with satisfaction.

"I'm very pleased."

"But I know that when you go away I will be troubled about your reality. You are a vision, a hallucination. Consequently I am physically ill, I am not normal."

"And what of that! Why are you troubled? You are ill because you have worked beyond your strength and you are exhausted, which means that you have sacrificed your health to an idea, and the time is near when you will sacrifice your life to it too. What could be better? It is the object to which all noble natures, gifted from above, constantly aspire."

"If I know that I am mentally diseased, can I believe in myself?"

"How do you know that the men of genius, who are believed in by the whole world, have not also seen visions? Scholars say now that genius is allied to insanity. My friend, only the ordinary people—the herd—are quite well and normal. All this consideration about the nervous century, overwork, degeneration, etc., can only seriously alarm those whose object in life is the present—that is the people of the herd."

"The Romans said: 'mens sana in corpore sano.'"

"Not all that the Romans and Greeks said is true. Overstrain, excitement, ecstasy, all that distinguishes the prophets, the poets, the martyrs for ideas, from ordinary people, is opposed to the animal side of man's nature, that is, to his physical health. I repeat, if you wish to be healthy and normal go to the herd."

"It is strange, you say what often comes into my mind," Kovrin said. "You appear to have looked into my soul and listened to my most secret thoughts. But let us not speak of me. What do you mean by the eternal truth?"

The monk did not reply. Kovrin glanced at him and could not distinguish his face. The features became misty and melted away. The monk's head and hands gradually disappeared, his body seemed to be blended with the bench and with the evening twilight and then he vanished entirely.

"The hallucination is over," Kovrin said, and he laughed. "What a pity!"

He returned towards the house gay and happy. What little the black monk had said to him flattered not only his self-love, but his whole soul, his whole being. To be one of the chosen, to serve the eternal truth, to stand in the ranks of those who will render mankind worthy of the Kingdom of God a few thousand years sooner than it would otherwise have been, that is, will save mankind from an extra thousand years of struggle, sin and suffering, to sacrifice everything—youth, strength, health, to the idea—to be ready to die for the general good— what a high, what a happy fate! His clean, chaste life, so full of work, passed through his memory; he remembered what he himself had learned, what he had taught others, and he arrived at the conclusion that there was no exaggeration in the words the monk had spoken.

Tania came to meet him through the park. She was dressed in another frock.

"Here you are at last!" she said. "We are looking for you everywhere. But what has happened to you?" she said with astonishment, gazing at his enraptured, beaming countenance and his eyes that were brimming over with tears. "How strange you look, Andryusha."

"I am satisfied, Tania," Kovrin said, putting his hands on her shoulders. "I am more than satisfied, I am happy! Tania, dear Tania, you are a most congenial creature! Dear Tania, I am so glad, so glad!"

He kissed both her hands passionately and continued:

"I have just passed through bright, beautiful, unearthly moments. But I cannot tell you all because you would call me mad, or you would not believe me. Let us talk of you. Dear, charming Tania! I love you, and I have become used to love you. Your nearness, our meetings, ten times daily have become a necessity for my soul. I don't know how I shall be able to exist without you, when I go home."

"Well!" and Tania laughed, "you will forget us in two days. We are little people, and you are a great man."

"No, let us talk seriously," he said. "I will take you with me. Yes? Won't you come with me? You want to be mine?"

"Well, well!" Tania said and again she wanted to laugh, but laughter would not come, and red spots came out on her face.

She began to breathe fast, and she walked on very quickly, not towards the house, but deeper into the park.

"I never thought of this . . . never!" she said, clasping her hands as if in despair.

Kovrin followed her and continued to speak with the same brilliant, excited face.

"I want love that would conquer me entirely, and that love, Tania, you alone can give me. I am happy, happy!"

She was stupefied, she bent, she shrivelled, she seemed suddenly to grow ten years older, and he thought her beautiful and he expressed his thoughts aloud:

"How beautiful she is!"

CHAPTER VI

The Black Guest

WHEN EGOR SEMENYCH heard from Kovrin that the romance had not only begun, but that there was to be a wedding, he walked about the rooms for a long time trying to hide his agitation. His hands began to tremble, his neck seemed to grow thicker and became purple; he ordered his racing droshky* to be put to and drove off somewhere. Tania, seeing how he whipped the horse and how low down, almost over his ears, he had pressed his cap, understood his mood, shut herself up in her room and cried all day.

The peaches and plums were already ripening in the hot-houses; the packing and sending off to Moscow of these delicate and tender goods required much attention, trouble and work. Owing to the summer having been very hot and dry, it was necessary to water every tree; this took up much time and labour; besides multitudes of caterpillars appeared on the trees, which the work-people, as well as Egor Semenych and Tania, crushed with their fingers, to Kovrin's great disgust. Besides all this work it was necessary to accept orders for fruit and trees for the autumn deliveries, and to carry on a large correspondence. While at the

*[Light carriage.]

busiest time, when it seemed that nobody had a moment to spare, the season for field work came on and took away more than half the hands from the garden. Egor Semenych, very much sunburnt, exhausted and irritated, rushed about now in the gardens, now in the fields, crying that he was torn to pieces, and that he would send a bullet through his head.

There was also all the bustle caused by the preparation of the trousseau, on which the Pesotskis set great store; everybody in the house was made quite dizzy by the click of scissors, the noise of sewing machines, the fumes of hot irons and the caprices of the milliner, a nervous lady, who was easily offended. And, as if on purpose, every day saw the arrival of guests, who had to be entertained and fed, and who often even stayed the night. However, all this drudgery passed by almost unperceived as if in a mist. Tania felt that love and happiness had come upon her unawares, although for some reason from the age of fourteen she had been convinced that Kovrin would be sure to marry her. She was amazed, she was perplexed, she could not believe it herself. . . . At times she was suddenly overpowered by such joy, that she wanted to fly above the clouds, and pray to God there; at others, equally suddenly, she would remember that in August she would have to take leave of her paternal home and her father, or—God knows from where the thought would come—that she was insignificant, small and unworthy of such a great man as Kovrin—then she went to her own room, locked herself in and wept bitterly during several hours. When they had company it would suddenly appear to her that Kovrin was uncommonly handsome, and that all the women were in love with him, and were envious of her; then her soul was filled with pride and delight as if she had conquered the whole world, but he had only to smile affably at one of the girls to cause her to tremble with jealousy and retire to her own room; then there were tears again. These new sensations quite took possession of her; she helped her father mechanically, and never noticed the peaches nor the caterpillars, nor the labourers, nor even how quickly the time flew.

Much the same happened to Egor Semenych. He worked from morning to night, he was always hurrying somewhere, he constantly lost his temper, he was irritable, but all this took place in a sort of enchanted state of semi-sleep. It was as if there were two men in him: one was the real Egor Semenych who, listening to his gardener, Ivan Karlych, making his report about the disorders in the gardens, would be indignant, and put his hands to his head in despair; and the other, not the real one, who, as if in a half-tipsy state, would suddenly break into the business report in the middle of a word and placing his hand on the gardener's shoulder would begin to murmur:

"Whatever one may say there is much in blood. His mother was a wonderful, a most noble, a most clever woman. It was a delight to look at her good, bright, pure face, like an angel's. She painted beautifully, she wrote verses, she could speak five foreign languages, she sang. . . . Poor thing, may the heavenly kingdom be hers, she died of consumption."

The unreal Egor Semenych sighed, and after a pause continued:

"When he was a boy growing up in my house, he had the same angelic, bright and good face. He has the same look, the same movements and the same soft, elegant manner of speaking that his mother had. And his intellect! He always astonished us by his intellect. By the way, it is not for nothing that he is a Master of Arts! . . . No, not for nothing! But wait a little, Ivan Karlych, you'll see what he'll be in ten years! He'll be quite unapproachable!"

But here the real Egor Semenych, checking himself, made a serious face, caught hold of his head and shouted:

"Devils! They've dirtied, destroyed, devastated everything! The garden is lost! The garden is ruined!"

Kovrin worked with the same zeal as before, and did not notice the hurly-burly around him. Love only added oil to the fire. After each meeting with Tania he returned to his room happy, enraptured, and with the same passion with which he had just kissed Tania and had told her of his love, he seized a book or set to work at his manuscript. All that the black monk had said about the chosen of God, eternal truth, the brilliant future of the human race, etc., only gave his work a special, an uncommon meaning and filled his soul with pride, and the consciousness of his own eminence. Once or twice a week either in the park or in the house he met the black monk and conversed with him for a long time; but this did not frighten him; on the contrary, it delighted him, as he was firmly convinced that such an apparition only visited the chosen, the eminent people, who had devoted themselves to the service of the idea.

One day the monk appeared during dinner and sat down in the dining-room near the window. Kovrin was delighted, and he very adroitly turned the conversation with Egor Semenych and Tania upon subjects that might interest the monk. The black guest listened and nodded his head affably; Egor Semenych and Tania also listened and smiled gaily, never suspecting that Kovrin was not talking to them, but to his vision.

Unperceived the fast of the Assumption was there, and soon after it the wedding-day arrived. The marriage was celebrated according to

Egor Semenych's persistent desire "with racket," that is, with senseless festivities that lasted two days. They ate and drank far more than three thousand roubles, but owing to the bad hired band, the shrill toasts, the hurrying to and fro of the lackeys, the noise and the overcrowding, nobody could appreciate the bouquet of the expensive wines nor the taste of the wonderful delicacies that had been ordered from Moscow.

CHAPTER VII

Don't Be Afraid!

IT HAPPENED on one of the long winter nights that Kovrin was lying in bed reading a French novel. Poor little Tania, who was not yet accustomed to live in a town, had a bad headache, as she often had by the evening, and was long since asleep, but from time to time she was uttering disconnected phrases in her sleep.

It had struck three. Kovrin blew out his candle and lay down. He lay long with closed eyes, but could not get to sleep, because (so it seemed to him) it was very hot in the bedroom and Tania was talking in her sleep. At half-past four he again lit the candle, and at that moment he saw the black monk sitting on the arm-chair that stood near the bed.

"How do you do?" the monk said, and after a short pause he asked: "Of what are you thinking now?"

"Of fame," Kovrin answered. "In the French novel I have just been reading there is a man, a young scientist, who did stupid things, and who pined away from longing for fame. These longings are incomprehensible to me."

"Because you are wise. You look upon fame with indifference, like a plaything that does not interest you."

"Yes, that is true."

"Fame has no attraction for you. What is there flattering, interesting or instructive in the fact that your name will be carved on your gravestone, and then time will efface this inscription together with its gilding? Besides, happily you are too many for man's weak memory to be able to remember all your names."

"Naturally," Kovrin agreed. "Why should they be remembered? But let us speak of something else. For example, of happiness. What is happiness?"

When the clock struck five he was sitting on his bed with his feet resting on the rug and turning to the monk he was saying:

"In ancient times one happy man was at last frightened at his own happiness—it was so great! And in order to propitiate the gods he sacrificed to them his most precious ring. You know that story? Like Polycrates, I am beginning to be alarmed at my own happiness. It appears to me strange that from morning to night I only experience joy; I am filled with joy and it smothers all other feelings. I do not know what sadness, grief or dullness is. Here am I not asleep. I suffer from sleeplessness, but I am not dull. Quite seriously, I'm beginning to be perplexed."

"Why?" the monk asked in astonishment. "Is joy a superhuman feeling? Ought it not to be the normal condition of man? The higher a man is in his intellectual and moral development, the more free he is, the greater are the pleasures that life offers him. Socrates, Diogenes and Marcus Aurelius knew joy, and not grief. The apostle says: 'Rejoice always.' Therefore rejoice and be happy."

"What if suddenly the gods were angered?" Kovrin said jokingly, and he laughed. "What if they take from me my comfort and make me suffer cold and hunger, it will scarcely be to my taste."

In the meantime Tania had awaked and looked at her husband with amazement and terror. He was talking, addressing himself to the armchair, gesticulating and laughing; his eyes glistened and there was something strange in his laughter.

"Andryusha, with whom are you talking?" she asked, catching hold of the hand he was stretching out to the monk. "Andryusha, with whom? . . ."

"Eh? With whom?" Kovrin became confused. "With him. There he sits," he answered, pointing to the black monk.

"There's nobody here . . . nobody! Andryusha, you're ill!"

Tania put her arms round her husband and pressed close to him, and as if to protect him from visions she put her hand over his eyes. "You are ill!" She sobbed and her whole body trembled. "Forgive me, darling, my dear one; I have long noticed that your soul is troubled about something. You are mentally ill, Andryusha. . . ."

Her shivering fit was communicated to him. He looked again at the armchair, which was now empty; he suddenly felt a weakness in the arms and legs, he was alarmed and began to dress.

"It's nothing, Tania, nothing . . ." he mumbled, shivering. "I really feel a little out of sorts . . . it's time to admit it."

"I have long noticed it—and papa has noticed it too," she said, trying to restrain her sobs. "You talk to yourself, you smile in a strange way . . . you don't sleep. Oh, my God, my God, save us!" she said in terror. "But you must not be afraid, Andryusha, don't be afraid, for God's sake, don't be afraid. . . ."

She also began to dress. Only now, when he looked at her, Kovrin understood all the danger of his position, he understood what the black monk and his talks with him meant. It was now quite clear to him that he was a madman.

They both dressed, without knowing why, and went into the drawing-room. She went first, he followed her. Here Egor Semenych, who was staying with them, was already standing in his dressing-gown with a candle in his hand.

"Don't be afraid, Andryusha," Tania said again, trembling like one with a fever. "Don't be afraid. Papa, it will soon pass, it will soon pass."

Kovrin was too excited to be able to speak. He wanted to say to his father-in-law in a playful tone:

"Congratulate me, I think I'm out of my mind," but his lips only moved, and he smiled bitterly.

At nine o'clock in the morning he was wrapped up in a fur coat and a shawl and driven in a carriage to the doctor's. He began a cure.

Chapter VIII

Torture

SUMMER HAD COME back again, and the doctor ordered Kovrin to go to the country. Kovrin was already cured, he had ceased seeing the black monk, and it only was necessary to restore his physical strength. While living on his father-in-law's estate he drank much milk, he worked only two hours a day, he did not drink wine, nor did he smoke.

On the eve of St. Elias's day vespers were celebrated in the house. When the deacon handed the censer to the priest there was an odour of the churchyard in the whole of the huge old hall, and it made Kovrin feel dull. He went into the garden. He walked about there without noticing the magnificent flowers; he sat on one of the benches and then wandered into the park; when he came to the river he went down to the water's edge and stood there for some time plunged in thought looking at the water. The gloomy pines, with their rough roots that but a year ago had seen him so young, joyful and hale, now did not whisper together, but stood motionless and dumb, just as if they did not recognize him. And, really, he was changed since last year; his head was closely cropped, his long beautiful hair was gone, his gait was languid, his face had grown stouter and paler.

He crossed over the foot-bridge to the other bank. Where the year before there had been rye, now mowed-down oats lay in long rows. The sun had already disappeared, and on the horizon the red glow of sunset was still widespread, foretelling wind for the next day. It was quiet. Looking in the direction where a year before the black monk had made his first appearance, Kovrin stood for about twenty minutes till the brightness of the sunset had faded away.

When he returned to the house languid and dissatisfied, vespers were over. Egor Semenych and Tania were sitting on the steps of the terrace drinking tea. They were talking about something, but when they saw Kovrin coming they suddenly were silent, and he concluded, judging by their faces, that the conversation had been about him.

"I think it's time for you to have your milk," Tania said to her husband.

"No, it's not time . . ." he answered as he sat down on the very lowest step. "Drink it yourself. I don't want it."

Tania exchanged an anxious glance with her father and said in a guilty tone:

"You yourself have noticed that milk does you good."

"Oh yes, very much good," Kovrin said, smiling. "I congratulate you; since Friday I have added another pound to my weight." He squeezed his head tightly between his hands and said sadly: "Why, why do you make me have this cure? All sorts of bromate preparations, idleness, warm baths, watching, poor-spirited, alarm for every mouthful, for every step—all this in the end will make a perfect idiot of me. I went mad, I had the mania of greatness, but for all that I was gay, healthy and even happy; I was interesting and original. Now I have become more sober-minded and matter-of-fact, but in consequence I am now like everybody else. I am mediocre, life is tiresome to me. . . . Oh, how cruelly you have acted towards me! I saw hallucinations; in what way did that interfere with anybody? I ask you, with whom did that interfere?"

"God knows what you are saying!" Egor Semenych said with a sigh. "It's tiresome to listen to you!"

"Then don't listen."

The presence of people, especially of Egor Semenych, irritated Kovrin. He answered him drily, coldly, even rudely, and when he looked at him it was always with derision and with hatred. Egor Semenych was confused and coughed guiltily, although he could feel no blame. Unable to understand this sudden and sharp change in their friendly and kind-hearted relations, Tania pressed close to her father, and looked into his eyes with troubled glances; she wanted to understand the cause, but could not; all that was clear to her was that their relations became with every day worse and worse, that latterly her father had aged very much, and that her husband had become irritable, capricious, quarrelsome and uninteresting. She could no longer laugh and sing, she ate nothing at dinner, she often had sleepless nights, expecting something dreadful, and she was so worn out that once she lay in a faint from dinner-time until evening. During vespers it had appeared to her that her father was crying, and now when they were all three sitting together on the terrace she had to make an effort not to think of this.

"How happy were Buddha, Mohammed and Shakespeare, that their kind relations and doctors did not try to cure them of their ecstasies and inspirations!" Kovrin said. "If Mohammed had taken bromide to calm his nerves, had worked only two hours a day and had drunk milk, as little would have remained of this remarkable man as of his dog. The doctors and the kind relations will in the end so blunt the capacities of mankind that at last mediocrity will be considered genius and civilization will perish. If you only knew how thankful I am to you!" Kovrin said with vexation.

He felt greatly irritated and to prevent himself from saying too much he rose quickly and went into the house. The night was calm, and the scent of tobacco and jalap was borne through the open window. In the large dark ballroom the moonlight lay in green patches on the floor and on the piano. Kovrin remembered his raptures of the previous summer, when the jalaps smelt in the same way and the moon looked in at the windows. In order to renew last year's frame of mind he hurried into his study, lit a strong cigar and ordered the butler to bring him some wine. But the cigar only left an unpleasantly bitter taste in his mouth, and the wine had not the same flavour it had had the year before. What loss of habit does! He got giddy from the cigar, and after two sips of wine he had palpitations of the heart, so he had to take a dose of bromide.

When she was going to bed Tania said to him:

"My father adores you. You are angry with him for some reason and it is killing him. Only look at him: he is ageing not by days, but by hours. I implore you, Andryusha, for God's sake, for the sake of your late father, for the sake of my peace, be more affectionate with him."

"I can't, and I won't."

"But why?" Tania asked, beginning to tremble all over. "Tell me why?"

"Because I don't like him, that's all," Kovrin said carelessly, and shrugged his shoulders; "but let us not talk of him, he is your father."

"I can't, I really can't understand," Tania said, pressing her hands to her temples and looking at a point in front of her. "Something incomprehensible, something terrible is happening in our house. You are changed, you are not like yourself. You are clever, you are no ordinary man and you get irritated with trifles; you meddle in all sort of tittle-tattle. Such trifles agitate you, that sometimes one is astonished and cannot believe it, and asks oneself: Is it you? Well, well, don't be angry, don't be angry," she continued, alarmed by her own words and kissing his hands. "You are clever, kind, noble. You will be towards with my father. He is so good."

"He's not good, but good-natured. The good-natured uncles in farces, who are somewhat like your father—well-fed and with good-natured faces, extremely hospitable and a little comical—appeared touching and amusing to me in novels and farces and also in real life at one time—now they are repugnant to me. They are all egoists to the marrow of their bones. What's most repugnant to me is their being overfed and their abdominal, their entirely oxlike or swinelike optimism."

Tania sat down on the bed and laid her head on the pillow.

"This is torture," she said, and her voice showed she was quite exhausted, and that it was difficult for her to speak. "Ever since the winter there has not been a single quiet moment. Good God, it is terrible! I suffer . . ."

"Yes, of course, I am Herod, and you and your little papa are the Egyptian infants. Oh, of course!"

His face appeared to Tania to be ugly and disagreeable; hatred and an expression of derision did not become him. For some time she had noticed there was something wanting in his face; it was as if a change had taken place in his countenance ever since the time his hair had been cut. She wanted to say something insulting to him, but at the moment she caught herself having such inimical feelings that she became alarmed and left the bedroom.

CHAPTER IX

Blood of Kovrin

KOVRIN WAS APPOINTED to a professor's chair. His inaugural address was announced for the second of December, and the notice of this lecture was hung up in the corridor of the University. But on the appointed day he sent a telegram to inform the provost that owing to illness he was unable to give the lecture.

He had had a severe hæmorrhage from the throat. For some time he had spat blood, but about twice a month the hæmorrhage was considerable, and after these attacks he experienced great weakness and fell into a somnolent condition. This illness did not cause him any special anxiety, as he knew that his mother had lived for ten years and even longer with exactly the same malady, and the doctors assured him that there was no danger; they advised him only to be calm, to live a regular life and to talk as little as possible.

In January he was again unable to give the lecture owing to the same cause, and in February it was already too late to begin the course, and it had to be postponed until the next year.

At that time he no longer lived with Tania, but with another woman, who was two years older than he was, and who looked after him as if he were a child. His frame of mind was peaceful and tranquil: he obeyed willingly, and when Varvara Nikolaevna decided to take him to the Crimea he consented, although he had a foreboding that nothing good would come of this journey.

They arrived in Sevastopol towards evening and stayed the night at an hotel to rest before proceeding the next day to Yalta. They were both exhausted from the long journey. Varvara Nikolaevna had some tea, went to bed and was soon sound asleep. But Kovrin remained up. An hour before leaving home he had received a letter from Tania, and he had not been able to make up his mind to open it; it was still lying in his side pocket, and the thought of its being there agitated him unpleasantly. In the depths of his soul he now quite sincerely considered his marriage to have been a mistake; he was glad that he had definitely separated from her, and the remembrance of that woman, who at last had turned into a live walking skeleton and in whom all appeared to be dead with the exception of the large clever eyes that looked steadily at you—aroused in him nothing but pity and sorrow for himself, and the handwriting on the envelope reminded him how unjust and cruel he had been two years ago, how he had vented his own voidness of soul, dullness, solitude and dissatisfaction with life on quite innocent people. This also reminded him of how one day he had torn into small pieces his dissertation and all the articles he had written during his illness and how he had thrown them out of the window, and the scraps of paper, blown about by the wind, had fluttered on to the flowers and the trees: in each line he saw strange pretensions that were founded on nothing, hare-brained passions, insolence, the mania of greatness, and this had produced on him the effect of reading a description of his own vices; but when the last copy-book had been torn up and had flown out of the window for some reason he had suddenly become sorry and embittered, and he had gone to his wife and had told her all sorts of unpleasant things. Good God, how he had pestered her! One day, wanting to cause her pain, he had told her that her father had played an unenviable part in their romance as he had asked him to marry her. Egor Semenych, who had accidentally overheard this, rushed into the room and in his despair was unable to utter a word; he only stood there shifting from one foot to another and uttering a strange lowing sound as if he had been deprived of the power of speech, and Tania, gazing at her father, gave a piercing shriek, and fell down in a swoon. It was disgraceful!

All this recurred to his memory at the sight of the familiar handwriting. Kovrin went out on to the balcony; it was a calm warm evening, and there was a scent of the sea. The moon and lights were reflected in the beautiful bay, which was of a colour for which it was difficult to find a name. It was a delicate and soft blending of blue and green; in places the water assumed the colour of green copperas, and in other places it seemed as if the moonlight had solidified, and instead of water had filled the bay, and in general what harmony of colour there was all around, what a peaceful, calm and lofty enjoyment!

In the floor below, just under the balcony, the window was probably open, because one could distinctly hear women's voices and laughter. It was evident an evening party was going on there.

Kovrin made an effort, unsealed the letter and reentering his room he read:

"My father has just died. I owe this to you as you have killed him. Our garden is ruined; strangers are now masters there; that is to say, what my poor father so feared is happening. I owe this to you too. I hate you with my whole soul, and I hope you will soon perish. Oh, how I suffer. My soul is consumed by unbearable pain. May you be accursed. I mistook you for an extraordinary man, for a genius. I loved you, but you proved to be a madman. . . ."

Kovrin could read no farther, he tore up the letter and threw it away. He was overpowered by a feeling of uneasiness that was almost like fear. Varvara Nikolaevna was sleeping behind the screen, and he could hear her breathing; from the story below the sound of women's voices and laughter were borne to him, but he had a sort of feeling that in the whole of the hotel there was not a living soul besides himself. Because unhappy, sorrowing Tania had cursed him in her letter, and had wished him to perish, a feeling of dread came over him, and he looked furtively at the door as if he feared that the unknown power, which in the space of some two years had caused such ruin in his life and in the lives of those dearest to him, would enter the room and again take possession of him.

By experience he knew that when his nerves were unstrung the best remedy was work. He must sit down to the table and force himself to concentrate his mind on some special subject. He took out of his portfolio a copy-book in which he had jotted down the synopsis of a small compilatory work he had thought of writing if the weather proved to be bad in the Crimea, as it was dull to be without occupation. He sat down to the table and began to work at this synopsis, and it appeared to him that his old peaceful, submissive, equitable frame of mind was coming back. The copy-book with the synopsis aroused in him thoughts of worldly vanities. He thought how much life takes for the insignificant or very ordinary blessings that it is able to give man in exchange. For example, in order to receive before forty an ordinary professorial chair, and to expound in a languid, tiresome, heavy style very ordinary thoughts, which besides are the thoughts of other people—in a word, to attain the position of a moderately good scholar, he, Kovrin, had to study for fifteen years, to work day and night, pass through serious mental disease, to survive an unsuccessful marriage and commit all sorts of follies and injustices, which it would be pleasant to forget. Kovrin realized now quite plainly that he was an ordinary mediocrity and he was quite satisfied with this, as he considered every man must be contented with what he was.

His synopsis would have been able to calm him if the white scraps of the torn-up letter that lay on the floor had not prevented him from concentrating his thoughts. He rose from the table, collected the fragments of the letter and threw them out of the window; but a light wind was blowing from the sea and the scraps of paper were scattered on the window-sill. He again was seized by a feeling of uneasiness that was almost like fear, and it seemed to him that in the whole of the hotel with the exception of himself there was not a single living soul. . . . He went on to the balcony. The bay, as if alive, looked at him with numberless azure, dark blue, turquoise-blue and fiery eyes and enticed him towards itself. It was really hot and sultry, and it would be pleasant to have a bath.

Suddenly in the lower story just under the balcony there was the sound of a violin and two delicate women's voices began to sing. They were singing something very familiar. The song that was being sung below told of a girl who had a sick imagination, who heard mysterious sounds at night in the garden, and made up her mind that they were sacred harmonies that were incomprehensible to us mortals. . . . Kovrin had catchings of his breath and his heart grew heavy with sadness, and a beautiful sweet joy, such as he had long forgotten, throbbed in his breast.

A high black column that looked like a whirlwind or a water-spout appeared on the opposite shores of the bay. With terrible rapidity it moved across the bay in the direction of the hotel, becoming smaller and darker, and Kovrin had scarcely time to stand to one side to make room for it. . . . A monk with a bare head and black eyebrows, barefooted, with hands crossed on his breast, was borne past him and stopped in the middle of the room.

"Why did you not believe me?" he asked reproachfully, and looked kindly at Kovrin. "If you had believed me then, when I told you that you were a genius, you would not have passed these two years so sadly and so miserably."

Kovrin believed that he was the chosen of God and a genius, he instantly remembered all his former conversations with the black monk, and he wanted to speak but blood began to flow from his throat straight on to his breast, and he, not knowing what to do, passed his hands over his chest and his cuffs became saturated with blood. He wanted to call Varvara Nikolaevna, who was sleeping behind the screen; he made an effort and said:

"Tania!"

He fell on the floor and raising himself on his arm again called:

"Tania!"

He called to Tania, he called to the great gardens with their lovely flowers sprinkled with dew, he called to the park, to the pines with their rugged roots, to the fields of rye, to his wonderful science, to his youth, courage, joy, he called to life that was so beautiful. He saw on the floor close to his face a large pool of blood, and from weakness he could not utter another word, but an inexpressible, a boundless happiness filled his whole being. Below, just under the balcony, they were playing the serenade, and the black monk whispered to him that he was a genius and that he was only dying because his weak human body had lost its balance and could no longer serve as the garb for a genius.

When Varvara Nikolaevna awoke and came from behind the screen Kovrin was already dead and his face had stiffened in a blissful smile.

The House with the Mezzanine

(A Painter's Story)

IT HAPPENED NIGH on seven years ago, when I was living in one of the districts of the J. province, on the estate of Bielokurov, a landowner, a young man who used to get up early, dress himself in a long overcoat, drink beer in the evenings, and all the while complain to me that he could nowhere find any one in sympathy with his ideas. He lived in a little house in the orchard, and I lived in the old manor-house, in a huge pillared hall where there was no furniture except a large divan, on which I slept, and a table at which I used to play patience. Even in calm weather there was always a moaning in the chimney, and in a storm the whole house would rock and seem as though it must split, and it was quite terrifying, especially at night, when all the ten great windows were suddenly lit up by a flash of lightning.

Doomed by fate to permanent idleness, I did positively nothing. For hours together I would sit and look through the windows at the sky, the birds, the trees and read my letters over and over again, and then for hours together I would sleep. Sometimes I would go out and wander aimlessly until evening.

Once on my way home I came unexpectedly on a strange farmhouse. The sun was already setting, and the lengthening shadows were thrown over the ripening corn. Two rows of closely planted tall fir-trees stood like two thick walls, forming a sombre, magnificent avenue. I climbed the fence and walked up the avenue, slipping on the fir needles which lay two inches thick on the ground. It was still, dark, and only here and there in the tops of the trees shimmered a bright gold light casting the colours of the rainbow on a spider's web. The smell of the firs was almost suffocating. Then I turned into an avenue of limes. And here too were desolation and decay; the dead leaves rustled mournfully beneath my feet, and there were lurking shadows among the trees. To the right, in an old orchard, a goldhammer sang a faint reluctant song, and he too

30

must have been old. The lime-trees soon came to an end and I came to a white house with a terrace and a mezzanine, and suddenly a vista opened upon a farmyard with a pond and a bathing-shed, and a row of green willows, with a village beyond, and above it stood a tall, slender belfry, on which glowed a cross catching the light of the setting sun. For a moment I was possessed with a sense of enchantment, intimate, particular, as though I had seen the scene before in my childhood.

By the white-stone gate surmounted with stone lions, which led from the yard into the field, stood two girls. One of them, the elder, thin, pale, very handsome, with masses of chestnut hair and a little stubborn mouth, looked rather prim and scarcely glanced at me; the other, who was quite young—seventeen or eighteen, no more, also thin and pale, with a big mouth and big eyes, looked at me in surprise, as I passed, said something in English and looked confused, and it seemed to me that I had always known their dear faces. And I returned home feeling as though I had awoke from a pleasant dream.

Soon after that, one afternoon, when Bielokurov and I were walking near the house, suddenly there came into the yard a spring-carriage in which sat one of the two girls, the elder. She had come to ask for subscriptions to a fund for those who had suffered in a recent fire. Without looking at us, she told us very seriously how many houses had been burned down in Sianov, how many men, women, and children had been left without shelter, and what had been done by the committee of which she was a member. She gave us the list for us to write our names, put it away, and began to say good-bye.

"You have completely forgotten us, Piotr Petrovich," she said to Bielokurov, as she gave him her hand. "Come and see us, and if Mr. N. (she said my name) would like to see how the admirers of his talent live and would care to come and see us, then mother and I would be very pleased."

I bowed.

When she had gone Piotr Petrovitch began to tell me about her. The girl, he said, was of a good family and her name was Lydia Volchaninov, and the estate, on which she lived with her mother and sister, was called, like the village on the other side of the pond, Sholkovka. Her father had once occupied an eminent position in Moscow and died a privy councillor. Notwithstanding their large means, the Volchaninovs always lived in the village, summer and winter, and Lydia was a teacher in the Zemstvo* School at Sholkovka and earned twenty-five roubles a month. She only spent what she earned on herself and was proud of her independence.

*[Local elective assembly.]

"They are an interesting family," said Bielokurov. "We ought to go and see them. They will be very glad to see you."

One afternoon, during a holiday, we remembered the Volchaninovs and went over to Sholkovka. They were all at home. The mother, Ekaterina Pavlovna, had obviously once been handsome, but now she was stouter than her age warranted, suffered from asthma, was melancholy and absent-minded as she tried to entertain me with talk about painting. When she heard from her daughter that I might perhaps come over to Sholkovka, she hurriedly called to mind a few of my landscapes which she had seen in exhibitions in Moscow, and now she asked what I had tried to express in them. Lydia, or as she was called at home, Lyda, talked more to Bielokurov than to me. Seriously and without a smile, she asked him why he did not work for the Zemstvo and why up till now he had never been to a Zemstvo meeting.

"It is not right of you, Piotr Petrovich," she said reproachfully. "It is not right. It is a shame."

"True, Lyda, true," said her mother. "It is not right."

"All our district is in Balaguin's hands," Lyda went on, turning to me. "He is the chairman of the council and all the jobs in the district are given to his nephews and brothers-in-law, and he does exactly as he likes. We ought to fight him. The young people ought to form a strong party; but you see what our young men are like. It is a shame, Piotr Petrovich."

The younger sister, Genya, was silent during the conversation about the Zemstvo. She did not take part in serious conversations, for by the family she was not considered grown-up, and they gave her her baby name, Missyuss, because as a child she used to call her English governess that. All the time she examined me curiously and when I looked at the photograph-album she explained: "This is my uncle. . . . That is my godfather," and fingered the portraits, and at the same time touched me with her shoulder in a childlike way, and I could see her small, undeveloped bosom, her thin shoulders, her long, slim waist tightly drawn in by a belt.

We played croquet and lawn-tennis, walked in the garden, had tea, and then a large supper. After the huge pillared hall, I felt out of tune in the small cosy house, where there were no oleographs on the walls and the servants were treated considerately, and everything seemed to me young and pure, through the presence of Lyda and Missyuss, and everything was decent and orderly. At supper Lyda again talked to Bielokurov about the Zemstvo, about Balaguin, about school libraries. She was a lively, sincere, serious girl, and it was interesting to listen to her, though she spoke at length and in a loud voice—perhaps because she was used to holding forth at school. On the other hand, Piotr Petrovich, who from his university days had retained the habit of reducing any conversation to a discussion, spoke tediously, slowly, and deliberately, with an obvious desire to be taken for a clever and progressive man. He gesticulated and upset the sauce with his sleeve and it made a large pool on the table-cloth, though nobody but myself seemed to notice it.

When we returned home the night was dark and still.

"I call it good breeding," said Bielokurov, with a sigh, "not so much not to upset the sauce on the table, as not to notice it when some one else has done it. Yes. An admirable intellectual family. I'm rather out of touch with nice people. Ah! terribly. And all through business, business, business!"

He went on to say what hard work being a good farmer meant. And I thought: What a stupid, lazy lout! When we talked seriously he would drag it out with his awful drawl—er, er, er—and he works just as he talks—slowly, always behindhand, never up to time; and as for his being businesslike, I don't believe it, for he often keeps letters given him to post for weeks in his pocket.

"The worst of it is," he murmured as he walked along by my side, "the worst of it is that you go working away and never get any sympathy from anybody."

II

I BEGAN TO FREQUENT the Volchaninovs' house. Usually I sat on the bottom step of the veranda. I was filled with dissatisfaction, vague discontent with my life, which had passed so quickly and uninterestingly, and I thought all the while how good it would be to tear out of my breast my heart which had grown so weary. There would be talk going on on the terrace, the rustling of dresses, the fluttering of the pages of a book. I soon got used to Lyda receiving the sick all day long, and distributing books, and I used often to go with her to the village, bareheaded, under an umbrella. And in the evening she would hold forth about the Zemstvo and schools. She was very handsome, subtle, correct, and her lips were thin and sensitive, and whenever a serious conversation started she would say to me drily:

"This won't interest you."

I was not sympathetic to her. She did not like me because I was a landscape-painter, and in my pictures did not paint the suffering of the masses, and I seemed to her indifferent to what she believed in. I remember once driving along the shore of the Baikal and I met a Bouryat girl, in shirt and trousers of Chinese cotton, on horseback: I asked her if she would sell me her pipe and, while we were talking, she looked with scorn at my European face and hat, and in a moment she got bored with talking to me, whooped and galloped away. And in exactly the same way Lyda despised me as a stranger. Outwardly she never showed her dislike of me, but I felt it, and, as I sat on the bottom step of the terrace, I had a certain irritation and said that treating the peasants without being a doctor meant deceiving them, and that it is easy to be a benefactor when one owns four thousand acres.

Her sister, Missyuss, had no such cares and spent her time in complete idleness, like myself. As soon as she got up in the morning she would take a book and read it on the terrace, sitting far back in a lounge chair so that her feet hardly touched the ground, or she would hide herself with her book in the lime-walk, or she would go through the gate into the field. She would read all day long, eagerly poring over the book, and only through her looking fatigued, dizzy, and pale sometimes, was it possible to guess how much her reading exhausted her. When she saw me come she would blush a little and leave her book, and, looking into my face with her big eyes, she would tell me of things that had happened, how the chimney in the servants' room had caught fire, or how the labourer had caught a large fish in the pond. On week-days she usually wore a bright-coloured blouse and a dark-blue skirt. We used to go out together and pluck cherries for jam, in the boat, and when she jumped to reach a cherry, or pulled the oars, her thin, round arms would shine through her wide sleeves. Or I would make a sketch and she would stand and watch me breathlessly.

One Sunday, at the end of June, I went over to the Volchaninovs in the morning about nine o'clock. I walked through the park, avoiding the house, looking for mushrooms, which were very plentiful that summer, and marking them so as to pick them later with Genya. A warm wind was blowing. I met Genya and her mother, both in bright Sunday dresses, going home from church, and Genya was holding her hat against the wind. They told me they were going to have tea on the terrace.

As a man without a care in the world, seeking somehow to justify his constant idleness, I have always found such festive mornings in a country house universally attractive. When the green garden, still moist with dew, shines in the sun and seems happy, and when the terrace smells of mignonette and oleander, and the young people have just returned from church and drink tea in the garden, and when they are all so gaily dressed and so merry, and when you know that all these healthy, satisfied, beautiful people will do nothing all day long, then you long for all life to be like that. So I thought then as I walked through the garden, quite prepared to drift like that without occupation or purpose, all through the day, all through the summer.

Genya carried a basket and she looked as though she knew that she would find me there. We gathered mushrooms and talked, and whenever she asked me a question she stood in front of me to see my face.

"Yesterday," she said, "a miracle happened in our village. Pelagueya, the cripple, has been ill for a whole year, and no doctors or medicines were any good, but yesterday an old woman muttered over her and she got better."

"That's nothing," I said. "One should not go to sick people and old women for miracles. Is not health a miracle? And life itself? A miracle is something incomprehensible."

"And you are not afraid of the incomprehensible?"

"No. I like to face things I do not understand and I do not submit to them. I am superior to them. Man must think himself higher than lions, tigers, stars, higher than anything in nature, even higher than that which seems incomprehensible and miraculous. Otherwise he is not a man, but a mouse which is afraid of everything."

Genya thought that I, as an artist, knew a great deal and could guess what I did not know. She wanted me to lead her into the region of the eternal and the beautiful, into the highest world, with which, as she thought, I was perfectly familiar, and she talked to me of God, of eternal life, of the miraculous. And I, who did not admit that I and my imagination would perish for ever, would reply: "Yes. Men are immortal. Yes, eternal life awaits us." And she would listen and believe me and never asked for proof.

As we approached the house she suddenly stopped and said:

"Our Lyda is a remarkable person, isn't she? I love her dearly and would gladly sacrifice my life for her at any time. But tell me"—Genya touched my sleeve with her finger—"but tell me, why do you argue with her all the time? Why are you so irritated?"

"Because she is not right."

Genya shook her head and tears came to her eyes.

"How incomprehensible!" she muttered.

At that moment Lyda came out, and she stood by the balcony with a riding-whip in her hand, and looked very fine and pretty in the sunlight as she gave some orders to a farm-hand. Bustling about and talking loudly, she tended two or three of her patients, and then with a businesslike, preoccupied look she walked through the house, opening one cupboard after another, and at last went off to the attic; it took some time to find her for dinner and she did not come until we had

finished the soup. Somehow I remember all these little details and love
to dwell on them, and I remember the whole of that day vividly, though
nothing particular happened. After dinner Genya read, lying in her
lounge chair, and I sat on the bottom step of the terrace. We were
silent. The sky was overcast and a thin fine rain began to fall. It was hot,
the wind had dropped, and it seemed the day would never end.
Ekaterina Pavlovna came out on to the terrace with a fan, looking very
sleepy.

"O, mamma," said Genya, kissing her hand. "It is not good for you to
sleep during the day."

They adored each other. When one went into the garden, the other
would stand on the terrace and look at the trees and call: "Hello!"
"Genya!" or "Mamma, dear, where are you?" They always prayed
together and shared the same faith, and they understood each other
very well, even when they were silent. And they treated other people in
exactly the same way. Ekaterina Pavlovna also soon got used to me and
became attached to me, and when I did not turn up for a few days she
would send to inquire if I was well. And she too used to look admiringly
at my sketches, and with the same frank loquacity she would tell me
things that happened, and she would confide her domestic secrets to
me.

She revered her elder daughter. Lyda never came to her for caresses,
and only talked about serious things: she went her own way and to her
mother and sister she was as sacred and enigmatic as the admiral, sitting
in his cabin, to his sailors.

"Our Lyda is a remarkable person," her mother would often say;
"isn't she?"

And, now, as the soft rain fell, we spoke of Lyda:

"She is a remarkable woman," said her mother, and added in a low
voice like a conspirator's as she looked round, "such as she have to be
looked for with a lamp in broad daylight, though you know, I am
beginning to be anxious. The school, pharmacies, books—all very well,
but why go to such extremes? She is twenty-three and it is time for her
to think seriously about herself. If she goes on with her books and her
pharmacies she won't know how life has passed. . . . She ought to
marry."

Genya, pale with reading, and with her hair ruffled, looked up and
said, as if to herself, as she glanced at her mother:

"Mamma, dear, everything depends on the will of God."

And once more she plunged into her book.

Bielokurov came over in a *poddiovka*,* wearing an embroidered shirt.

---

*[A long, close-fitting pleated coat.]

We played croquet and lawn-tennis, and when it grew dark we had a long supper, and Lyda once more spoke of her schools and Balaguin, who had got the whole district into his own hands. As I left the Volchaninovs that night I carried away an impression of a long, long idle day, with a sad consciousness that everything ends, however long it may be. Genya took me to the gate and, perhaps because she had spent the whole day with me from the beginning to end, I felt somehow lonely without her, and the whole kindly family was dear to me: and for the first time during the whole of that summer I had a desire to work.

"Tell me why you lead such a monotonous life," I asked Bielokurov, as we went home. "My life is tedious, dull, monotonous, because I am a painter, a queer fish, and have been worried all my life with envy, discontent, disbelief in my work: I am always poor, I am a vagabond, but you are a wealthy, normal man, a landowner, a gentleman—why do you live so tamely and take so little from life? Why, for instance, haven't you fallen in love with Lyda or Genya?"

"You forget that I love another woman," answered Bielokurov.

He meant his mistress Lyubov Ivanovna, who lived with him in the orchard house. I used to see the lady every day, very stout, podgy, pompous, like a fatted goose, walking in the garden in a Russian head-dress, always with a sunshade, and the servants used to call her to meals or tea. Three years ago she rented a part of his house for the summer, and stayed on to live with Bielokurov, apparently for ever. She was ten years older than he and managed him very strictly, so that he had to ask her permission to go out. She would often sob and make horrible noises like a man with a cold, and then I used to send and tell her that if she did not stop I would go away. Then she would stop.

When we reached home, Bielokurov sat down on the divan and frowned and brooded, and I began to pace up and down the hall, feeling a sweet stirring in me, exactly like the stirring of love. I wanted to talk about the Volchaninovs.

"Lyda could only fall in love with a Zemstvo worker like herself, some one who is run off his legs with hospitals and schools," I said. "For the sake of a girl like that a man might not only become a Zemstvo worker, but might even become worn out, like the tale of the iron boots. And Missyuss? How charming Missyuss is!"

Bielokurov began to talk at length and with his drawling er-er-ers of the disease of the century—pessimism. He spoke confidently and argumentatively. Hundreds of miles of deserted, monotonous, blackened steppe could not so forcibly depress the mind as a man like that, sitting and talking and showing no signs of going away.

"The point is neither pessimism nor optimism," I said irritably, "but that ninety-nine out of a hundred have no sense."

Bielokurov took this to mean himself, was offended, and went away.

III

"THE PRINCE is on a visit to Malozyomov and sends you his regards," said Lyda to her mother, as she came in and took off her gloves. "He told me many interesting things. He promised to bring forward in the Zemstvo Council the question of a medical station at Malozyomov, but he says there is little hope." And turning to me, she said: "Forgive me, I keep forgetting that you are not interested."

I felt irritated.

"Why not?" I asked and shrugged my shoulders. "You don't care about my opinion, but I assure you, the question greatly interests me."

"Yes?"

"In my opinion there is absolutely no need for a medical station at Malozyomov."

My irritation affected her: she gave a glance at me, half closed her eyes and said:

"What is wanted then? Landscapes?"

"Not landscapes either. Nothing is wanted there."

She finished taking off her gloves and took up a newspaper which had just come by post; a moment later, she said quietly, apparently controlling herself:

"Last week Anna died in childbirth, and if a medical man had been available she would have lived. However, I suppose landscape-painters are entitled to their opinions."

"I have a very definite opinion, I assure you," said I, and she took refuge behind the newspaper, as though she did not wish to listen. "In my opinion medical stations, schools, libraries, pharmacies, under existing conditions, only lead to slavery. The masses are caught in a vast chain: you do not cut it but only add new links to it. That is my opinion."

She looked at me and smiled mockingly, and I went on, striving to catch the thread of my ideas.

"It does not matter that Anna should die in childbirth, but it does matter that all these Annas, Marfas, Pelagueyas, from dawn to sunset should be grinding away, ill from overwork, all their lives worried about their starving sickly children; all their lives they are afraid of death and disease, and have to be looking after themselves; they fade in youth, grow old very early, and die in filth and dirt; their children as they grow up go the same way and hundreds of years slip by and millions of people

live worse than animals—in constant dread of never having a crust to
eat; but the horror of their position is that they have no time to think of
their souls, no time to remember that they are made in the likeness of
God; hunger, cold, animal fear, incessant work, like drifts of snow
block all the ways to spiritual activity, to the very thing that
distinguishes man from the animals, and is the only thing indeed that
makes life worth living. You come to their assistance with hospitals and
schools, but you do not free them from their fetters; on the contrary,
you enslave them even more, since by introducing new prejudices into
their lives, you increase the number of their demands, not to mention
the fact that they have to pay the Zemstvo for their drugs and
pamphlets, and therefore, have to work harder than ever."

"I will not argue with you," said Lyda. "I have heard all that." She
put down her paper. "I will only tell you one thing, it is no good sitting
with folded hands. It is true, we do not save mankind, and perhaps we
do make mistakes, but we do what we can and we are right. The highest
and most sacred truth for an educated being—is to help his neighbours,
and we do what we can to help. You do not like it, but it is impossible to
please everybody."

"True, Lyda, true," said her mother.

In Lyda's presence her courage always failed her, and as she talked
she would look timidly at her, for she was afraid of saying something
foolish or out of place: and she never contradicted, but would always
agree: "True, Lyda, true."

"Teaching peasants to read and write, giving them little moral
pamphlets and medical assistance, cannot decrease either ignorance or
mortality, just as the light from your windows cannot illuminate this
huge garden," I said. "You give nothing by your interference in the
lives of these people. You only create new demands, and a new
compulsion to work."

"Ah! My God, but we must do something!" said Lyda exasperatedly,
and I could tell by her voice that she thought my opinions negligible
and despised me.

"It is necessary," I said, "to free people from hard physical work. It
is necessary to relieve them of their yoke, to give them breathing space,
to save them from spending their whole lives in the kitchen or the byre,
in the fields; they should have time to take thought of their souls, of
God and to develop their spiritual capacities. Every human being's
salvation lies in spiritual activity—in his continual search for truth and
the meaning of life. Give them some relief from rough, animal labour,
let them feel free, then you will see how ridiculous at bottom your
pamphlets and pharmacies are. Once a human being is aware of his

vocation, then he can only be satisfied with religion, service, art, and not with trifles like that."

"Free them from work?" Lyda gave a smile. "Is that possible?"

"Yes. . . . Take upon yourself a part of their work. If we all, in town and country, without exception, agreed to share the work which is being spent by mankind in the satisfaction of physical demands, then none of us would have to work more than two or three hours a day. If all of us, rich and poor, worked three hours a day the rest of our time would be free. And then to be still less dependent on our bodies, we should invent machines to do the work and we should try to reduce our demands to the minimum. We should toughen ourselves and our children should not be afraid of hunger and cold, and we should not be anxious about their health, as Anna, Maria, Pelagueya were anxious. Then supposing we did not bother about doctors and pharmacies, and did away with tobacco factories and distilleries—what a lot of free time we should have! We should give our leisure to service and the arts. Just as peasants all work together to repair the roads, so the whole community would work together to seek truth and the meaning of life, and, I am sure of it—truth would be found very soon, man would get rid of his continual, poignant, depressing fear of death and even of death itself."

"But you contradict yourself," said Lyda. "You talk about service and deny education."

"I deny the education of a man who can only use it to read the signs on the public houses and possibly a pamphlet which he is incapable of understanding—the kind of education we have had from the time of Rurik: and village life has remained exactly as it was then. Not education is wanted but freedom for the full development of spiritual capacities. Not schools are wanted but universities."

"You deny medicine too."

"Yes. It should only be used for the investigation of diseases, as natural phenomena, not for their cure. It is no good curing diseases if you don't cure their causes. Remove the chief cause—physical labour, and there will be no diseases. I don't acknowledge the science which cures," I went on excitedly. "Science and art, when they are true, are directed not to temporary or private purposes, but to the eternal and the general—they seek the truth and the meaning of life, they seek God, the soul, and when they are harnessed to passing needs and activities, like pharmacies and libraries, then they only complicate and encumber life. We have any number of doctors, pharmacists, lawyers, and highly educated people, but we have no biologists, mathematicians, philosophers, poets. All our intellectual and spiritual energy is wasted

on temporary passing needs. . . . Scientists, writers, painters work and
work, and thanks to them the comforts of life grow greater every day,
the demands of the body multiply, but we are still a long way from the
truth and man still remains the most rapacious and unseemly of
animals, and everything tends to make the majority of mankind
degenerate and more and more lacking in vitality. Under such
conditions the life of an artist has no meaning and the more talented he
is, the more strange and incomprehensible his position is, since it only
amounts to his working for the amusement of the predatory, disgusting
animal, man, and supporting the existing state of things. And I don't
want to work and will not. . . . Nothing is wanted, so let the world go to
hell."

"Missyuss, go away," said Lyda to her sister, evidently thinking my
words dangerous to so young a girl.

Genya looked sadly at her sister and mother and went out.

"People generally talk like that," said Lyda, "when they want to
excuse their indifference. It is easier to deny hospitals and schools than
to come and teach."

"True, Lyda, true," her mother agreed.

"You say you will not work," Lyda went on. "Apparently you set a
high price on your work, but do stop arguing. We shall never agree,
since I value the most imperfect library or pharmacy, of which you
spoke so scornfully just now, more than all the landscapes in the
world." And at once she turned to her mother and began to talk in quite
a different tone: "The Prince has got very thin, and is much changed
since the last time he was here. The doctors are sending him to Vichy."

She talked to her mother about the Prince to avoid talking to me. Her
face was burning, and, in order to conceal her agitation, she bent over
the table as if she were short-sighted and made a show of reading the
newspaper. My presence was distasteful to her. I took my leave and
went home.

IV

ALL WAS QUIET outside: the village on the other side of the pond was
already asleep, not a single light was to be seen, and on the pond there
was only the faint reflection of the stars. By the gate with the stone
lions stood Genya, waiting to accompany me.

"The village is asleep," I said, trying to see her face in the darkness,
and I could see her dark sad eyes fixed on me. "The innkeeper and the
horse-stealers are sleeping quietly, and decent people like ourselves
quarrel and irritate each other."

It was a melancholy August night—melancholy because it already

smelled of the autumn: the moon rose behind a purple cloud and hardly
lighted the road and the dark fields of winter corn on either side. Stars
fell frequently, Genya walked beside me on the road and tried not to
look at the sky, to avoid seeing the falling stars, which somehow
frightened her.

"I believe you are right," she said, trembling in the evening chill. "If
people could give themselves to spiritual activity, they would soon
burst everything."

"Certainly. We are superior beings, and if we really knew all the
power of the human genius and lived only for higher purposes then we
should become like gods. But this will never be. Mankind will
degenerate and of their genius not a trace will be left."

When the gate was out of sight Genya stopped and hurriedly shook
my hand.

"Good night," she said, trembling; her shoulders were covered only
with a thin blouse and she was shivering with cold. "Come to-morrow."

I was filled with a sudden dread of being left alone with my inevitable
dissatisfaction with myself and people, and I, too, tried not to see the
falling stars.

"Stay with me a little longer," I said. "Please."

I loved Genya, and she must have loved me, because she used to meet
me and walk with me, and because she looked at me with tender
admiration. How thrillingly beautiful her pale face was, her thin nose,
her arms, her slenderness, her inactivity, her constant reading. And
her mind? I suspected her of having an unusual intellect: I was
fascinated by the breadth of her views, perhaps because she thought
differently from the strong, handsome Lyda, who did not love me.
Genya liked me as a painter, I had conquered her heart by my talent,
and I longed passionately to paint only for her, and I dreamed of her as
my little queen, who would one day possess with me the trees, the
fields, the river, the dawn, all Nature, wonderful and fascinating, with
whom, as with them, I have felt hopeless and useless.

"Stay with me a moment longer," I called. "I implore you."

I took off my overcoat and covered her childish shoulders. Fearing
that she would look queer and ugly in a man's coat, she began to laugh
and threw it off, and as she did so, I embraced her and began to cover
her face, her shoulders, her arms with kisses.

"Till to-morrow," she whispered timidly as though she was afraid to
break the stillness of the night. She embraced me: "We have no secrets
from one another. I must tell mamma and my sister. . . . Is it so
terrible? Mamma will be pleased. Mamma loves you, but Lyda!"

She ran to the gates.

"Good-bye," she called out.

For a couple of minutes I stood and heard her running. I had no desire to go home, there was nothing there to go for. I stood for a while lost in thought, and then quietly dragged myself back, to have one more look at the house in which she lived, the dear, simple, old house, which seemed to look at me with the windows of the mezzanine for eyes, and to understand everything. I walked past the terrace, sat down on a bench by the lawn-tennis court, in the darkness under an old elm-tree, and looked at the house. In the windows of the mezzanine, where Missyuss had her room, shone a bright light, and then a faint green glow. The lamp had been covered with a shade. Shadows began to move. . . . I was filled with tenderness and a calm satisfaction, to think that I could let myself be carried away and fall in love, and at the same time I felt uneasy at the thought that only a few yards away in one of the rooms of the house lay Lyda who did not love me, and perhaps hated me. I sat and waited to see if Genya would come out. I listened attentively and it seemed to me they were sitting in the mezzanine.

An hour passed. The green light went out, and the shadows were no longer visible. The moon hung high above the house and lit the sleeping garden and the avenues: I could distinctly see the dahlias and roses in the flower-bed in front of the house, and all seemed to be of one colour. It was very cold. I left the garden, picked up my overcoat in the road, and walked slowly home.

Next day after dinner when I went to the Volchaninovs', the glass door was wide open. I sat down on the terrace expecting Genya to come from behind the flower-bed or from out of the rooms; then I went into the drawing-room and the dining-room. There was not a soul to be seen. From the dining-room I went down a long passage into the hall, and then back again. There were several doors in the passage and behind one of them I could hear Lyda's voice:

"To the crow somewhere . . . God . . ."—she spoke slowly and distinctly, and was probably dictating—". . . God sent a piece of cheese . . . To the crow . . . somewhere . . . Who is there?" she called out suddenly as she heard my footsteps.

"It is I."

"Oh! excuse me. I can't come out just now. I am teaching Masha."

"Is Ekaterina Pavlovna in the garden?"

"No. She and my sister left today for my Aunt's in Penza, and in the winter they are probably going abroad." She added after a short silence: "To the crow somewhere God sent a pi-ece of cheese. Have you got that?"

I went out into the hall, and, without a thought in my head, stood and looked out at the pond and the village, and still I heard:

"A piece of cheese . . . To the crow somewhere God sent a piece of cheese."

And I left the house by the way I had come the first time, only reversing the order, from the yard into the garden, past the house, then along the lime-walk. Here a boy overtook me and handed me a note: "I have told my sister everything and she insists on my parting from you," I read. "I could not hurt her by disobeying. God will give you happiness. If you knew how bitterly mamma and I have cried."

Then through the fir avenue and the rotten fence. . . . Over the fields where the corn was ripening and the quails screamed, cows and shackled horses now were browsing. Here and there on the hills the winter corn was already showing green. A sober, workaday mood possessed me and I was ashamed of all I had said at the Volchaninovs', and once more it became tedious to go on living. I went home, packed my things, and left that evening for Petersburg.

I never saw the Volchaninovs again. Lately on my way to the Crimea I met Bielokurov at a station. As of old he was in a *poddiovka*, wearing an embroidered shirt, and when I asked after his health, he replied: "Quite well, thanks be to God." He began to talk. He had sold his estate and bought another, smaller one in the name of Lyubov Ivanovna. He told me a little about the Volchaninovs. Lyda, he said, still lived at Sholkovka and taught the children in the school. Little by little she succeeded in gathering round herself a circle of sympathetic people, who formed a strong party, and at the last Zemstvo election they drove out Balaguin, who up till then had had the whole district in his hands. Of Genya Bielokurov said that she did not live at home and he did not know where she was.

I have already begun to forget about the house with the mezzanine, and only now and then, when I am working or reading, suddenly— without rhyme or reason—I remember the green light in the window, and the sound of my own footsteps as I walked through the fields that night, when I was in love, rubbing my hands to keep them warm. And even more rarely, when I am sad and lonely, I begin already to recollect and it seems to me that I, too, am being remembered and waited for, and that we shall meet. . . .

Missyuss, where are you?

The Peasants

CHAPTER I

Blows

NIKOLAI TCHIKILDEYEFF, WAITER, of the Slaviansky Bazaar Hotel at Moscow, became ill. Once in a corridor he stumbled and fell with a tray of ham and peas and had to resign. What money he had, his own and his wife's, soon went on treatment. He was tired of idleness and had to return to his native village. It was cheaper to live at home, after all, and the best place for invalids; and there is some truth in the proverb, "At home the walls feel good."

He arrived at Zhukovo towards evening. He pictured his birthplace as cosy, and comfortable as a child, but now when he entered the hut he knew it was close, and dirty inside. And his wife Olga and little daughter Sasha looked questioningly at the big, sooty stove, black from smoke, which took up half the hut and was covered with flies. The stove was crooked, the logs in the walls sloped, and it seemed that every minute the hut would tumble to pieces. The ikon-corner, instead of pictures, was hung with bottle-labels and newspaper-cuttings. Poverty, poverty! Of the grown-ups no one was at home—they reaped in the fields; and alone on the stove sat an eight-year-old girl, fair-haired, unwashed, and so indifferent that she did not even look at the strangers. Beneath, a white cat rubbed herself against the pot-hanger.

"Puss, puss!" cried Sasha. "Pussy!"

"She can't hear," said the girl on the stove. "She's deaf!"

"How deaf?"

"Deaf. . . . From beating."

The first glance told Nikolai and Olga the life awaiting them; but they said nothing, silently laid down their bundles, and went into the street. The hut was the third from the corner, and the oldest and poorest in sight; its next-door neighbour, indeed, was little better; but the corner cabin boasted an iron roof and curtains in the windows. This cabin had no fence, and stood alone; it was the village inn. In one continuous row stretched other huts; and, as a whole, the village, peaceful and meditative, with the willows, elders, and mountain-ash peeping out of the gardens, was pleasing to see.

Behind the cabins the ground sloped steeply towards the river; and here and there in the clay stuck denuded stones. On the slope, around these stones and the potters' pits, lay heaps of potsherds, some brown, some red; and below stretched a broad, flat, and bright green meadow, already mown, and now given over to the peasants' herds. A verst* from the village ran the winding river with its pretty tufted banks; and beyond the river another field, a herd, long strings of white geese; then, as on the village side, a steep ascent. On the crest of the hill rose another village with a five-cupolaed church, and a little beyond it the local noble's house.

"It's a fine place, your village," said Olga, crossing herself towards the church. "What freedom, Lord!"

At that moment (it was Saturday night) the church bells rang for vesper service. In the valley beneath, two little girls with a water-pail turned their heads towards the church and listened to the bells.

"At the Slaviansky Bazaar they're sitting down to dinner," said Nikolai thoughtfully.

Seated on the brink of the ravine, Nikolai and Olga watched the setting sun and the image of the gold and purple sky in the river and in the church windows, and inhaled the soft, restful, inexpressibly pure air, unknown to them in Moscow. When the sun had set came lowing cattle and bleating sheep; geese flew towards them; and all was silent. The soft light faded from the air and evening shadows swept across the land.

Meantime the absent family returned to the hut. First came Nikolai's father and mother, dry, bent, and toothless, and of equal height. Later, their sons' wives, Marya and Fekla, employed on the noble's farm across the river. Marya, wife of Nikolai's brother Kiriak, had six children; Fekla, wife of Denis, then a soldier, two; and when Nikolai, entering the hut, saw the whole family, all these big and little bodies, which moved in the loft, in cradles, in corners; when he saw the greed with which the old man and women ate black bread soaked in water, he felt that he had made a mistake in coming home, sick, penniless, and—what was worse—with his family.

"And where is brother Kiriak?" he asked, greeting his parents.

"He's watchman at the trader's," answered the old man. "In the wood. He's a good lad, but drinks heavily."

"He's no profit," said the old woman in a lachrymose voice. "Our

*[See page 1.]

men are not much use, they bring nothing home with them, and only take things. Our Kiriak drinks; and the old man, there's no use hiding it, himself knows the way to the drink-shop. They've angered our Mother in Heaven!"

In honor of the guests the samovar was brought out. The tea smelt of fish, the sugar was damp and looked as if it had been gnawed, the bread and vessels were covered with cockroaches; it was painful to drink, and painful to hear the talk—of nothing but poverty and sickness. Before they had emptied their first glasses, from the yard came a loud drawling, drunken cry—

"Ma-arya!"

"That sounds like Kiriak," said the old man. "Talk of the devil and he appears!"

The peasants were silent. A moment later came the same cry, rough and drawling, and this time it seemed to come from underground.

"Ma-arya!"

The elder daughter-in-law, Marya, turned deadly pale and pressed her body to the stove; and it was strange to see the expression of terror on the face of this strong, broad-shouldered, ugly woman. Her daughter, the little, indifferent girl who had sat on the stove, suddenly began to cry loudly.

"Stop howling, cholera!" cried angrily Fekla, a good-looking woman, also strong and broad-shouldered. "He won't kill you!"

From the old man Nikolai soon learned that Marya was afraid to live with her husband in the forest; and that when he had drunk too much Kiriak came for her, and made scenes and beat her mercilessly.

"Ma-arya!" came the cry, this time from outside the door.

"Help me, for the love of heaven, help me!" chattered Marya, breathing as if she had been thrown into icy water. "Help me, kinsmen——"

The houseful of children suddenly began to cry, and, seeing them, Sasha did the same. A drunken cough echoed without, and into the hut came a tall, black-bearded muzhik* wearing a winter cap. In the dim lamp-light his face was barely visible, and all the more terrible. It was Kiriak. He went straight to his wife, flourished his arm, and struck her with his clenched fist in the face. Marya did not utter a sound, the blow seemed to have stunned her, but she seemed to dwindle; a stream of blood flowed out of her nose.

"It's a shame, a shame," muttered the old man, climbing on the stove. "And before our visitors! It's a sin!"

*[Peasant.]

The old woman kept silence, and, bent in two, seemed lost in thought. Fekla rocked the cradle. Kiriak seized Marya's hand, dragged her to the door, and, to increase her terror, roared like a beast. But at that moment he saw the visitors, and stopped.

"So you've come!" he began, releasing his wife. "My own brother and his family. . . ."

He prayed a moment before the image, staggered, opened his red, drunken eyes, and continued—

"My brother and family have come to their parents' house . . . from Moscow, that means . . . The old capital, that means, the city of Moscow, mother of cities. . . . Excuse . . ."

Amid the silence of all, he dropped on the bench near the samovar, and began to drink loudly from a saucer. When he had drunk ten cupfuls he leaned back on the bench and began to snore.

Bed-time came. Nikolai, as an invalid, was given a place on the stove beside the old man; Sasha slept on the floor; and Olga went with the young women to the shed.

"Never mind, my heart!" she said, lying on the hay beside Marya. "Crying is no help. You must bear it. In the Bible it is written, 'Whosoever shall smite thee on thy right cheek, turn to him the other also.' Don't cry, my heart!"

And then, in a whisper, she began to tell of Moscow, of her life there, how she had served as housemaid in furnished lodgings.

"In Moscow the houses are big and built of brick," said Olga. "There is no end of churches—forty forties of them—my heart; and the houses are all full of gentlemen, so good-looking, so smart!"

And Marya answered that she had never been in the district town, much less in Moscow; she was illiterate, and knew no prayers, not even "Our Father." Both she and her sister-in-law Fekla, who sat some way off and listened, were ignorant in the extreme, and understood nothing. Both disliked their husbands; Marya dreaded Kiriak, shook with terror when he stayed with her, and after his departure her head ached from the smell of vodka and tobacco. And Fekla, in answer to the question did she want her husband, answered angrily—

"What? . . . Him?"

For a time the women spoke, and then lay down.

It was cold, and a cock crew loudly, hindering sleep. When the blue morning light began to break through the chinks, Fekla rose stealthily and went out, and her movements could be heard, as she ran down the street in her bare feet.

CHAPTER II

Marya

WHEN OLGA went to church she took with her Marya. As they descended the path to the meadow, both were in good humour. Olga liked the freedom of the country; and Marya found in her sister-in-law a kindred spirit. The sun was rising. Close to the meadow flew a sleepy hawk; the river was dull, for there was a slight mist, but the hill beyond it was bathed in light; the church glittered, and rooks cawed in the garden of the big house beyond.

"The old man is not bad," said Marya. "But my mother-in-law is cross and quarrelsome. Our own corn lasted till Shrovetide; now we have to buy at the inn; and the old woman is angry, and says, 'You eat too much.'"

"Never mind, my heart! You must bear that too. It is written in the Bible, 'Come unto Me all ye that are weary and heavy laden.'"

Olga spoke gravely and slowly; and walked, like a pilgrim, quickly and briskly. Every day she read the Gospel, aloud, like a clerk; and though there was much that she did not understand, the sacred words touched her to tears, and words like *astche, dondezhe** she pronounced with beating heart. She believed in God, in the Virgin, in the saints; and her faith was that it was wrong to do evil to any man, even to Germans, gipsies, and Jews. When she read aloud the Gospel, even when she stopped at words she did not understand, her face grew compassionate, kindly, and bright.

"What part are you from?" asked Marya.

"Vladimir. I have been long in Moscow, since I was eight years old."

They approached the river. On the other bank stood a woman, undressing herself.

"That is our Fekla!" said Marya. "She's been across the river at the squire's house. With the stewards! She's impudent and ill-spoken—awful!"

Black-browed Fekla, with loosened hair, jumped into the river, and, young and firm as a girl, splashed in the water, making big waves.

"She's impudent—awful!" repeated Marya.

Across the river was a shaky bridge of beams, and at that moment beneath it in the clear, transparent water swam carp. On the green bushes, imaged in the water, glistened dew. It was warm and pleasant.

*[Words in Church Slavonic, the liturgical language.]

What a wonderful morning! And indeed, how splendid would be life in this world were it not for poverty, hideous, hopeless poverty, from which there is no escape! But look back to the village, and memory awakens all the events of yesterday; and the intoxication of joy vanishes in a wink.

The women reached the church. Marya stopped near the door, afraid to go inside. She feared, too, to sit down, though the service would not begin till nine o'clock, and stood all the time.

As the Gospel was being read the worshippers suddenly moved, and made way for the squire's family. In came two girls in white dresses with wide-brimmed hats, and behind them a stout, rosy boy dressed as a sailor. Their coming pleased Olga; she felt that here at last were well-taught, orderly, good-looking people. But Marya looked at them furtively and gloomily, as if they were not human beings but monsters who would crush her if she failed to make way.

And when the deacon sang out in a bass voice, she fancied she heard the cry "Ma-arya!" and shuddered.

CHAPTER III

Songs

THE VILLAGE quickly heard of the visitors' arrival, and when church was over the hut was crowded. The Leonuitcheffs, Matveitcheffs, and Ilitchoffs came for news of their kinsmen in Moscow. Every man in Zhukovo who could read and write was taken to Moscow as waiter or boots; and, similarly, the village across the river supplied only bakers; and this custom obtained since before the Emancipation, when a certain legendary Luka Ivanuitch, of Zhukovo, was lord of the buffet in a Moscow club, and hired none but fellow-villagers. These, in turn attaining power, sent for their kinsmen and found them posts in inns and restaurants; so that from that time Zhukovo was called by the local population Khamskaya or Kholuefka.† Nikolai was taken to Moscow at the age of eleven, and given a post by Ivan Makaruitch, one of the Matveitcheffs, then porter at the Hermitage Gardens. And, now, turning to the Matveitcheffs, Nikolai said gravely—

"Ivan Makaruitch was my benefactor; it is my duty to pray God for him day and night, for it was through him I became a good man."

"*Batiushka** mine!" said tearfully a tall, old woman, Ivan Makaruitch's sister. "And have you no news of him?"

*["Little father." *Batiushki*, which occurs later, is the plural.]
†[Jocular names implying that inn personnel are cads and toadies.]

"He was at Omon's last winter; and this season, I heard, he's in some gardens outside town. . . . He's grown old. Once in the summer he'd bring home ten roubles a day, but now everywhere business is dull—the old man's in a bad way."

The women, old and young, looked at the high felt boots on Nikolai's legs, and at his pale face, and said sadly—

"You're no money-maker, Nikolai Osipuitch, no money-bringer!"

And all caressed Sasha. Sasha was past her tenth birthday, but, small and very thin, she looked not more than seven. Among the sunburnt, untidy village girls, in their long cotton shirts, pale-faced, big-eyed Sasha, with the red ribbon in her hair, seemed a toy, a little strange animal caught in the fields, and brought back to the hut.

"And she knows how to read!" boasted Olga, looking tenderly at her daughter. "Read something, child!" she said, taking a New Testament from the corner. "Read something aloud and let the orthodox listen!"

The old, heavy, leather-bound, bent-edged Bible smelt like a monk. Sasha raised her eyebrows, and began in a loud drawl—

". . . And when they were departed, behold the angel of the Lord appeareth to Joseph in a dream, saying, Arise and take the young child and his mother . . ."

"'The young child and his mother,'" repeated Olga. She reddened with joy.

". . . and flee into Egypt . . . and be thou there until I bring thee word. . . ."

At the word "until" Olga could not longer restrain her emotion and began to cry. Marya followed her example, and Ivan Makaruitch's sister cried also. The old man coughed and fussed about, seeking a present for his grandchild, but he found nothing, and waved his hand. When the reading ended, the visitors dispersed to their homes, deeply touched, and pleased with Olga and Sasha.

As the day was Sunday the family remained in the hut. The old woman, whom husband, daughters-in-law, and grandchildren alike addressed as "grandmother," did everything with her own hands: she lighted the stove, set the samovar; she even worked in the fields; and at the same time growled that she was tortured with work. She tortured herself with dread that the family might eat too much, and took care that her husband and daughters-in-law did not sit with idle hands. Once when she found that the innkeeper's geese had got into her kitchen-garden, she rushed at once out of the house armed with a long stick; and for half an hour screamed piercingly over her cabbages, which were as weak and thin as their owner. Later she imagined that a hawk had swooped on her chickens, and with loud curses she flew to meet the hawk. She lost her temper and growled from morning to night, and often screamed so loudly that passers-by stopped to listen.

Her husband she treated badly, denouncing him sometimes as a lie-abed, sometimes as "cholera." The old man was a hopeless, unsubstantial muzhik, and perhaps, indeed, if she had not spurred him on, he would have done no work at all, but sat all day on the stove and talked. He complained to his son at great length of certain enemies in the village and of the wrongs he suffered day by day; and it was tiresome to hear him.

"Yes," he said, putting his arms to his waist. "Yes. A week after Elevation I sold my hay for thirty kopeks a pood. Yes. Good! . . . and this means that one morning I drive my hay cart and interfere with nobody; and suddenly, in an evil moment, I look round, and out of the inn comes the headman, Antip Siedelnikoff. 'Where are you driving, old So-and-so?' and bangs me in the ear!"

Kiriak's head ached badly from drink, and he was ashamed before his brother.

"It's drink that does it. *Akh*, my Lord God!" he stammered, shaking his big head. "You, brother, and you, sister, forgive me, for the love of Christ; I feel bad myself."

To celebrate Sunday, they bought herrings at the inn, and made soup of the heads. At midday all sat down to tea and drank until they sweated and, it seemed, swelled up; and when they had drunk the tea they set to on the soup, all eating from the same bowl. The old woman hid away the herrings.

At night a potter baked his pots in the ravine. In the meadow below, the village girls sang in chorus; and some one played a concertina. Beyond the river also glowed a potter's oven, and village girls sang; and from afar the music sounded soft and harmonious. The muzhiks gathered in the inn; they sang tipsily, each a different song; and the language they used made Olga shudder and exclaim—

"*Akh, batiushki!*"

She was astonished by the incessant blasphemy, and by the fact that the older men, whose time had nearly come, blasphemed worst of all. And the children and girls listened to this language, and seemed in no way uncomfortable; it was plain they were used to it, and had heard it from the cradle.

Midnight came; the potters' fires on both river-banks went out, but on the meadow below and in the inn the merry-making continued. The old man and Kiriak, both drunk, holding hands, and rolling against one another, came to the shed where Olga lay with Marya.

"Leave her alone!" reasoned the old man. "Leave her. She's not a bad sort. . . . It's a sin. . . ."

"Ma-arya!" roared Kiriak.

"Stop! It's sinful. . . . She's not a bad sort."

The two men stood a moment by the shed and went away.

"I love wild flowers . . ." sang the old man in a high, piercing tenor. "I love to pull them in the fields!"

After this he spat, blasphemed, and went into the hut.

CHAPTER IV

Dreams!

GRANDMOTHER STATIONED Sasha in the kitchen garden, and ordered her to keep off the geese. It was a hot August day. The innkeeper's geese could get into the kitchen garden by the back way, but at present they were busy picking up oats near the inn and quietly conversing, though the old gander stood aloof, his head raised as if to make sure that grandmother was not coming with her stick. The other geese could also get into the garden; but these were feeding far across the river, and, like a big white garland, stretched across the meadow. Sasha watched a short time, and then got tired, and, seeing no geese in sight, went down to the ravine.

There she saw Motka, Marya's eldest daughter, standing motionless on a big stone, and looking at the church. Marya had borne thirteen children; but only six remained, all girls, and the eldest was eight years old. Bare-footed Motka, in her long shirt, stood in the sun; the sun burnt the top of her head, but she took no notice of this, and seemed turned to stone. Sasha stood beside her, and looking at the church, began—

"God lives in the church. People burn lamps and candles, but God has red lamps, green and blue lamps, like eyes. At night God walks about the church, and with him the Holy Virgin, and holy Nicholas . . . toup, toup, toup! . . . The watchman is frightened, terribly! Yes, my heart," she said, imitating her mother. "When the Day of Judgment comes all the churches will be carried to heaven."

"With the bells?" asked Motka in a bass voice, drawling every word.

"With the bells. And on the Day of Judgment good people will go to paradise, and wicked people will burn in fire eternal and unextinguishable, my heart! To mother and Marya God will say, 'You have offended no one, so go to the right, to paradise'; but He'll say to Kiriak and grandmother, 'You go to the left, into the fire!' And people who eat meat on fast-days will go to the fire too."

She looked up at the sky, opened wide her eyes, and continued—

"Look up at the sky, don't wink . . . and you'll see angels."

Motka looked at the sky, and a minute passed in silence.

"Do you see them?" asked Sasha.

"No," answered Motka in her bass voice.

"But I can. Little angels fly about the sky, with wings . . . little, little, like gnats."

Motka thought, looked at the ground, and asked—

"Will grandmother burn really?"

"She'll burn, my heart."

From the stone to the bottom of the hill was a gentle, even slope covered with green grass so soft that it invited repose. Sasha lay down and slid to the bottom. Motka with a serious, severe face, puffed out her cheeks, lay down, and slid, and as she slid her shirt came up to her shoulders.

"How funny I felt!" said Sasha in delight.

The two children climbed to the top intending to slide down again, but at that moment they heard a familiar, squeaky voice. Terror seized them. Toothless, bony, stooping grandmother, with her short grey hair floating in the wind, armed with the long stick, drove the geese from the kitchen garden, and screamed—

"You've spoiled all the cabbage, accursed; may you choke; threefold anathemas; plagues, there is no peace with you!"

She saw the two girls, threw down her stick, took up a bundle of brushwood, and seizing Sasha's shoulders with fingers dry and hard as tree-forks, began to beat her. Sasha cried from pain and terror; and at that moment a gander, swinging from foot to foot and stretching out its neck, came up and hissed at the old woman; and when he returned to the geese, all welcomed him approvingly: go-go-go! Thereafter grandmother seized and whipped Motka, and again Motka's shirt went over her shoulders. Trembling with terror, crying loudly, Sasha went back to the hut to complain, and after her went Motka, also crying in her bass voice. Her tears were unwiped away, and her face was wet as if she had been in the river.

"Lord in heaven!" cried Olga as they entered the hut. "Mother of God, what's this?"

Sasha began her story, and at that moment, screaming and swearing, in came grandmother. Fekla lost her temper, and the whole hut was given over to noise.

"Never mind, never mind!" consoled Olga, pale and unnerved,

stroking Sasha's head. "She's your grandmother; you've no right to be angry. Never mind, child!"

Nikolai, already tortured by the constant shouting, hunger, smell, and smoke, hating and despising poverty, and ashamed of his parents before his wife and child, swung his legs over the stove and said to his mother with an irritable whine—

"You mustn't touch her! You have no right whatever to beat her!"

"*Nu,* you'll choke there on the stove, corpse!" cried Fekla angrily. "The devil sent you to us, parasite!"

And Sasha and Motka, and all the little girls, hid on the stove behind Nikolai's back, and the throbbing of their little hearts was almost heard. In every family with an invalid, long sick and hopeless, there are moments when all, timidly, secretly, at the bottom of their hearts, wish for his death; alone, children always dread the death of any one kin to them, and feel terror at the thought. And now the little girls, with bated breath and mournful faces, looked at Nikolai, and thinking that he would soon die, wanted to cry and say something kindly and compassionate.

Nikolai pressed close to Olga, as if seeking a defender, and said in a soft, trembling voice—

"Olga, my dear, I can stand this no longer. It is beyond my strength. For the love of God, for the love of Christ in heaven, write to your sister, Claudia Abramovna; let her sell or pledge everything, and send us the money to get out of this. O Lord," he cried, with longing, "to look at Moscow again, even with one eye! Even to see it in dreams!"

When evening came and the hut grew dark, all felt such tedium that it was hard to speak. Angry grandmother soaked rye crusts in a bowl, and took an hour to eat them. Marya milked the cow, carried in the milk-pail, and set it down on a bench; and grandmother slowly poured the milk into jugs, pleased at the thought that now at Assumption fast no one would drink milk, and that it would remain whole. But she poured a little, very little, into a saucer for Fekla's youngest. When she and Marya carried the milk to the cellar Motka suddenly started up, climbed down from the stove, and going to the bench poured the saucer of milk into the wooden bowl of crusts.

Grandmother, back in the hut, sat down again to the crusts, and Sasha and Motka, perched on the stove, looked at her, and saw with joy that she was drinking milk during fast time, and therefore would go to hell. Consoled by this, they lay down to sleep; and Sasha, going off to sleep, imagined the terrible chastisement: a big stove, like the potter's, and a black unclean spirit horned like a cow drove grandmother into the stove with a long stick, as she herself had lately driven the geese.

Anton Chekhov

CHAPTER V

Fire!

ON THE NIGHT of Assumption, at eleven o'clock, the young men and girls playing below in the meadow suddenly cried and shrieked and ran back towards the village. The boys and girls who sat above, on the brink of the ravine, at first could not understand the cause of their cries.

"Fire! Fire!" came from beneath in a despairing scream. "The hut's on fire!"

The boys and girls on the ravine turned their heads and saw a picture terrible and rare. Over one of the farthest thatched huts rose a fathom-high pillar of fire which curled and scattered fountain-wise on all sides showers of bright sparks. And immediately afterwards the whole roof caught fire, and the crackling of burning beams was heard by all.

The moonlight faded, and soon the whole village was bathed in a red, trembling glare; black shadows moved across the ground, and there was a smell of burning. The merry-makers from below, all panting, speechless, shuddering, jostled one another and fell; dazzled by the bright light, they saw nothing, and could not even tell who was who. The sight was terrible; and most terrible of all was that in the smoke above the conflagration fluttered doves, and that the men in the inn, knowing nothing of the fire, continued to sing and play the concertina as if nothing had happened.

"Uncle Semion is burning!" cried a loud, hoarse voice.

Marya with chattering teeth wandered about her hut weeping and wringing her hands, although the fire was far away at the other end of the village; Nikolai came out in his felt boots and after him the children in their shirts. At the village policeman's hut they beat the alarm. Bem, bem, bem! echoed through the air; and this tireless, repeated sound made the heart sink and the listeners turn cold. The old women stood about with images. From the yards were driven sheep, calves, and cows; and the villagers carried into the street their boxes, sheepskins, and pails. A black stallion, kept apart from the herd because he kicked and injured the horses, found himself in freedom, and neighing loudly, he tore up and down the village, and at last stopped beside a cart and kicked it violently.

In the church beyond the river the fire-alarm was rung.

It was hot all around the burning hut, and in the bright glare even the blades of grass were visible. On a box which the peasants had managed to save sat Semion, a big-nosed, red-headed muzhik, in short coat, with a forage-cap pressed down to his ears; his wife lay on her face on the earth and groaned. A little, big-bearded, capless, gnome-like stranger of eighty, evidently partial to fires, wandered around, carrying a white bundle; his bald head reflected the glare. The *starosta*,* Antip Siedelnikoff, swarthy and black-haired as a gipsy, went up to the hut with his axe, and for no apparent reason beat in all the windows and began to hack at the steps.

"Women, water!" he roared. "Bring the engine! Look sharp!"

The peasants, fresh from merry-making in the inn, dragged up the fire-engine. All were drunk; they staggered and fell; their expressions were helpless, and tears stood in their eyes.

"Bring water, girls!" cried the *starosta*, also drunk. "Look sharp!"

The young women and girls ran down the slope to the well, returned with pails and pitchers of water, and, having emptied them into the engine, ran back for more. Olga, and Marya, and Sasha, and Motka, all helped. The water was pumped up by women and small boys; the hose-nozzle hissed; and the *starosta*, aiming it now at the door, now at the windows, held his finger on the stream of water, so that it hissed still more fiercely.

"Good man, Antip!" came approving cries. "Keep it up!"

And Antip went into the hall and cried thence—

"Bring more water! Do your best, Orthodox men and women, on this unfortunate occasion!"

The muzhiks stood in a crowd with idle hands and gaped at the fire. No one knew what to start on, not one was capable of help; although around were stacks of grain, hay, outhouses, and heaps of dry brushwood. Kiriak and his father Osip, both tipsy, stood in the crowd. As if to excuse his idleness, the old man turned to the woman who lay on the ground and said—

"Don't worry yourself, gossip! The hut's insured—it's all the same to you!"

And Semion, addressing each muzhik in turn, explained how the hut caught fire.

"That old man there with the bundle is General Zhukoff's servant. . . . He was with our general, heaven kingdom to him! as cook. He comes up to us in the evening and begins, 'Let me sleep here tonight.' . . . We had a drink each, of course. . . . The woman prepared the samovar to get the old man tea, when in an unlucky moment she put it in the hall; and the fire from the chimney, of course,

*[Village head.]

went up to the roof, the straw and all! We were nearly burnt ourselves. And the old man lost his cap; it's a pity."

The fire-alarm boomed without cease; and the bells of the church across the river rang again and again. Olga, panting, bathed in the glare, looked with terror at the red sheep and the red pigeons flying about in the smoke; and it seemed to her that the boom of the fire-alarm pierced into her soul, that the fire would last for ever, and that Sasha was lost. . . . And when the roof crashed in she grew so weak with fear lest the whole village burn that she could no longer carry water; and she sat on the brink of the ravine with her pail beside her; beside her sat other women, and spoke as if they were speaking of a corpse.

At last from the manor-house came two cartloads of factors and workmen. They brought with them a fire-engine. A very youthful student in white, unbuttoned tunic rode into the village on horseback. Axes crashed, a ladder was placed against the burning log-walls; and up it promptly climbed five men led by the student, who was very red, and shouted sharply and hoarsely, and in a tone which implied that he was well accustomed to extinguishing fires. They took the hut to pieces, beam by beam; and dragged apart stall, the wattle fence, and the nearest hayrick.

"Don't let them break it!" came angry voices from the crowd. "Don't let them!"

Kiriak with a resolute face went into the hut as if to prevent the new-comers breaking, but one of the workmen turned him back with a blow on the neck. Kiriak tumbled, and on all fours crept back to the crowd.

From across the river came two pretty girls in hats; the student's sisters, no doubt. They stood some way off and watched the conflagration. The scattered logs no longer burned, but smoked fiercely; and the student, handling the hose, sent the water sometimes on the logs, sometimes into the crowd, sometimes at the women who were carrying pails.

"George!" cried the frightened girls reproachfully. "George!"

The fire ended. Before the crowd dispersed the dawn had begun; and all faces were pale and a little dark—or so it always seems in early morning when the last stars fade away. As they went to their homes the muzhiks laughed and joked at the expense of General Zhukoff's cook and his burnt cap: they reenacted the fire as a joke, and, it seemed, were sorry it had come so quickly to an end.

"You put out the fire beautifully, sir," said Olga to the student. "Quite in the Moscow way; there we have fires every day."

"Are you really from Moscow?" asked one of the girls.

"Yes. My husband served in the Slaviansky Bazaar. And this is my little girl." She pointed to Sasha, who pressed close to her from the cold. "Also from Moscow, miss."

The girls spoke to the student in French, and handed Sasha a twenty-kopeck piece. When old Osip saw this his face grew bright with hope.

"Thank God, your honour, there was no wind," he said, turning to the student. "We'd have been all burnt up in an hour. Your honour, good gentleman," he added shamefacedly. "It's a cold morning; we want warming badly . . . a half a bottle from your kindness . . ."

Osip's hint proved vain; and, grunting, he staggered home. Olga stood at the end of the village and watched as the two carts forded the stream, and the pretty girls walked through the meadow towards the carriage waiting on the other side. She turned to the hut in ecstasies—

"And such nice people! So good-looking. The young ladies, just like little cherubs!"

"May they burst asunder!" growled sleepy Fekla angrily.

CHAPTER VI

The Hut

MARYA WAS UNHAPPY, and said that she wanted to die. But life as she found it was quite to Fekla's taste: she liked the poverty, and the dirt, and the never-ceasing bad language. She ate what she was given without picking and choosing, and could sleep comfortably anywhere; she emptied the slops in front of the steps: threw them, in fact, from the threshold, though in her own naked feet she had to walk through the puddle. And from the first day she hated Olga and Nikolai for no reason save that they loathed this life.

"We'll see what you're going to eat here, my nobles from Moscow!" she said maliciously. "We'll see!"

Once on an early September morning, Fekla, rosy from the cold, healthy, and good-looking, carried up the hill two pails of water; when she entered the hut Marya and Olga sat at the table and drank tea.

"Tea . . . and sugar!" began Fekla ironically. "Fine ladies you are!" she added, setting down the pails. "A nice fashion you've got of drinking tea everyday! See that you don't swell up with tea!" she continued, looking with hatred at Olga. "You got a thick snout already in Moscow, fatbeef!"

She swung round the yoke and struck Olga on the shoulder. The two women clapped their hands and exclaimed—

"*Akh, batiushki!*"

After which Fekla returned to the river to wash clothes, and all the time cursed so loudly that she was heard in the hut.

The day passed, and behind it came the long autumn evening. All sat winding silk, except Fekla, who went down to the river. The silk was given out by a neighbouring factory; and at this work the whole family earned not more than twenty kopecks a week.

"We were better off as serfs," said the old man, winding away busily. "In those days you'd work, and eat, and sleep . . . each in its turn. For dinner you'd have *schtchi** and porridge, and for supper again *schtchi* and porridge. Gherkins and cabbage as much as you liked; and you'd eat freely, as much as you liked. And there was more order. Each man knew his place."

The one lamp in the hut burned dimly and smoked. When any worker rose and passed the lamp a black shadow fell on the window, and the bright moonlight shone in. Old Osip related slowly how the peasants lived before the Emancipation; how in these same villages where all to-day lived penuriously there were great shooting parties, and on such days the muzhiks were treated to vodka without end; how whole trains of carts with game for the young squire were hurried off to Moscow; how the wicked were punished with rods or exiled to the estate in Tver, and the good were rewarded. And grandmother also spoke. She remembered everything. She told of her old mistress, a good, God-fearing woman with a wicked, dissolute husband; and of the queer marriages made by all the daughters; one, it appeared, married a drunkard; another a petty tradesman; and the third was carried off clandestinely (she, grandmother, then unmarried, helped in the adventure): and all soon afterwards died of grief as did, indeed, their mother. And, remembering these events, grandmother began to cry.

When a knock was heard at the door all started.

"Uncle Osip, let me stay the night!"

Into the hut came the little, bald old man, General Zhukoff's cook, whose cap was burnt in the fire. He sat and listened, and, like his hosts, related many strange happenings. Nikolai, his legs hanging over the stove, listened; and asked what sort of food was eaten at the manor-house. They spoke of *bitki,*† cutlets, soups of various kinds, and sauces; and the cook, who, too, had an excellent memory, named certain dishes

*[Cabbage soup.]
†[Meat dumplings.]

which no one eats nowadays; there was a dish, for instance, made of
ox-eyes, and called "Awake in the morning."

"And did you cook cutlets *maréchal?*" asked Nikolai.

"No."

Nikolai shook his head reproachfully, and said—

"Then you are a queer sort of cook."

The little girls sat and lay on the stove, and looked down with widely
opened eyes; there seemed to be no end to them—like cherubs in the
sky. The stories delighted them; they sighed, shuddered, and turned
pale sometimes from rapture, sometimes from fear; and, breathless,
afraid to move, they listened to the stories of their grandmother, which
were the most interesting of all.

They went to bed in silence; and the old men, agitated by their
stories, thought how glorious was youth, which—however meagre it
might be—left behind it only joyful, living, touching recollections; and
how terribly cold was this death, which was now so near. Better not
think of it! The lamp went out. And the darkness, the two windows,
bright with moonshine, the silence, the cradle's creak somehow
reminded them that life was now past, and that it would never return.
They slumbered, lost consciousness; then suddenly some one jostled
their shoulders, or breathed into their cheeks—and there was no real
sleep; through their heads crept thoughts of death; they turned round
and forgot about death; but their heads were full of old, mean, tedious
thoughts, thoughts of need, of forage, of the rise in the price of flour;
and again they remembered that life had now passed by, and that it
would never return.

"O Lord!" sighed the cook.

Some one tapped cautiously at the window. That must be Fekla. Olga
rose, yawned, muttered a prayer, opened the inner door, then drew the
bolt in the hall. But no one entered. A draught blew and the moon shone
brightly. Through the open door, Olga saw the quiet and deserted
street, and the moon itself, swimming high in the sky.

"Who's there?" she cried.

"I!" came a voice. "It's I."

Near the door, pressing close to the wall, stood Fekla, naked as she
was born. She shuddered from the cold, her teeth chattered; and in the
bright moonlight she was pale, pretty, and strange. The patches of
shade and the moonlight on her skin stood out sharply; and plainest of
all stood out her dark eyebrows and her young, firm breast.

"Some impudent fellows across the river undressed me and sent
me off in this way—as my mother bore me! Bring me something to
put on."

"Go into the hut yourself!" whispered Olga, with a shudder.

"The old ones will see me."

And as a fact grandmother got restless, and growled; and the old man asked, "Who is there?" Olga brought out her shirt and petticoat and dressed Fekla; and the two women softly, and doing their best to close the doors without notice, went into the hut.

"So that's you, devil?" came an angry growl from grandmother, who guessed it was Fekla. "May you be . . . night walker . . . there's no peace with you!"

"Don't mind, don't mind," whispered Olga, wrapping Fekla up. "Don't mind, my heart!"

Again silence. The whole family always slept badly; each was troubled by something aggressive and insistent; the old man by a pain in the back; grandmother by worry and ill-temper; Marya by fright; the children by itching and hunger. And to-night the sleep of all was troubled; they rolled from side to side, wandered, and rose constantly to drink.

Fekla suddenly cried out in a loud, rough voice; but soon mastered herself, and merely sobbed quietly until at last she ceased. Now and then from beyond the river were heard the church chimes; but the clock struck strangely; and at first beat struck five, and later three.

"O Lord!" sighed the cook.

From the light in the windows it was hard to judge whether the moon still shone or whether dawn had come. Marya rose and went out; and she was heard milking the cows and shouting "Stand!" Grandmother also went out. It was still dark in the hut, but everything could be seen.

Nikolai, who had spent a sleepless night, climbed down from the stove. He took from a green box his evening dresscoat, put it on, and going over to the window, smoothed the sleeves and the folds, and smiled. Then he took off the coat, returned it to the box, and lay down.

Marya returned, and began to light the stove. Apparently she was not yet quite awake. Probably she still dreamed of something, or recalled the stories of last night, for she stretched herself lazily before the stove and said—

"No, we're better in freedom."

CHAPTER VII

Who Else?

IN THE VILLAGE arrived "the gentleman," as the peasants called the superintendent of police. Every one knew a week ahead the day and cause of his arrival. For though Zhukovo had only forty houses, it owed in arrears to the Imperial Treasury and the Zemstvo* more than two thousand roubles.

The superintendent stopped at the inn, drank two glasses of tea, and then walked to the *starosta's* hut, where already waited a crowd of peasants in arrears. The *starosta*, Antip Siedelnikoff, despite his youth—he was little over thirty—was a stern man who always took the side of the authorities, although he himself was poor and paid his taxes irregularly. It was clear to all that he was flattered by his position and revelled in the sense of power, which he had no other way of displaying save by sternness. The *mir*† feared and listened to him; when in the street or at the inn he met a drunken man he would seize him, tie his hands behind his back, and put him in the village gaol; once, indeed, he even imprisoned grandmother for several days, because, appearing at the *mir* instead of her husband, she used abusive language. The *starosta* had never lived in town and read no books; but he had a copious collection of learned words and used them so liberally that people respected him, even when they did not understand.

When Osip with his tax book entered the *starosta's* hut, the superintendent, a thin, old, grey-whiskered man in a grey coat, sat at a table in the near corner and made notes in a book. The hut was clean, the walls were decorated with pictures from magazines, and in a prominent place near the ikon hung a portrait of Alexander of Battenberg, ex-Prince of Bulgaria. At the table, with crossed arms, stood Antip Siedelnikoff.

"This man, your honour, owes 119 roubles," he said when it came to Osip's turn. "Before Holy Week, he paid a rouble, since then, nothing."

The superintendent turned his eyes on Osip, and asked—

"What's the reason of that, brother?"

"Your honour, be merciful to me . . ." began Osip in agitation. "Let me explain . . . this summer . . . Squire Liutoretzky . . . 'Osip,' he says, 'sell me your hay. . . . Sell it,' he says. . . . I had a hundred poods for sale, which the women mowed. . . . Well, we bargained. . . . All went well, without friction. . . ."

He complained of the *starosta*, and now and again turned to the muzhiks as if asking for support; his flushed face sweated, and his eyes turned bright and vicious.

"I don't understand why you tell me all that," said the superintendent. "I ask *you* . . . it's *you* I ask, why you don't pay your arrears? None of you pay, and I am held responsible."

"I'm not able to."

"These expressions are without consequence, your honour," said the *starosta* magniloquently. "In reality, the Tchikildeyeffs belong to the impoverished class, but be so good as to ask the others what is the reason. Vodka and impudence . . . without any comprehension."

The superintendent made a note, and said to Osip in a quiet, even voice, as if he were asking for water—

"Begone!"

Soon afterwards he drove away; and as he sat in his cheap tarantass* and coughed, it was plain, even from the appearance of his long, thin back, that he had forgotten Osip, and the *starosta,* and the arrears of Zhukovo, and was thinking of his own domestic affairs. He had hardly covered a verst before Antip Siedelnikoff was carrying off the Tchikildeyeff samovar; and after him ran grandmother, and whined like a dog.

"I won't give it! I won't give it to you, accursed!"

The *starosta* walked quickly, taking big steps; and grandmother, stooping and fierce and breathless, tottered after him; and her green-grey hair floated in the wind. At last she stopped, beat her breast with her fists, and exclaimed, with a whine and a sob—

"Orthodox men who believe in God! *Batiushki,* they're wronging me! Kinsmen, they've robbed me. Oi, oi, will no one help me!"

"Grandmother, grandmother!" said the *starosta* severely, "have some reason in your head!"

With the loss of the samovar, things in the Tchikildeyeffs' hut grew even worse. There was something humiliating and shameful in this last privation, and it seemed that the hut had suddenly lost its honour. The table itself, the chairs, and all the pots, had the *starosta* seized them, would have been less missed. Grandmother screamed, Marya cried, and the children, listening, began to cry also. The old man, with a feeling of guilt, sat gloomily in the corner and held his tongue. And Nikolai was silent. As a rule grandmother liked him and pitied him; but at this crisis her pity evaporated, and she cursed and reproached him, and thrust her fists under his nose. She screamed that he was guilty of the family's misfortunes and asked why he had sent so little home, though he boasted in his letters that he earned fifty roubles a month at the Slaviansky Bazaar. Why did he come home, and still worse, bring his family? If he died whence would the money come for his funeral? . . . And it was painful to look at Nikolai, Olga and Sasha.

The old man grunted, took his cap, and went to the *starosta's.* It was

*[Covered traveling wagon.]

getting dark. Antip Siedelnikoff, with cheeks puffed out, stood at the
stove and soldered. It was stifling. His children, skinny and unwashed—not better than the Tchikildeyeffs'—sprawled on the floor;
his ugly, freckled wife wound silk. This, too, was an unhappy, God-
forsaken family; alone Antip was smart and good-looking. On a bench
in a row stood five samovars. The old man prayed towards the
Battenberg prince, and began—

"Antip, show the mercy of God: give me the samovar! For the love of
God!"

"Bring me three roubles, and then you'll get it."

"I haven't got them."

Antip puffed out his cheeks, the fire hummed and hissed, and the
samovars shone. The old man fumbled with his cap, thought a moment,
and repeated—

"Give it to me!"

The swarthy *starosta* seemed quite black and resembled a wizard; he
turned to Osip and said roughly and quickly—

"All depends from the Rural Chief. In the administrative session of
the twenty-sixth of this month you can expose the causes of your
dissatisfaction verbally or in writing."

Not one of these learned words was understood by Osip, but he felt
contented, and returned to his hut.

Ten days later the superintendent returned, stayed about an hour,
and drove away. It had turned windy and cold, but though the river was
frozen, there was no snow, and the state of the roads was a torture to
every one. On Sunday evening the neighbours looked in to see and talk
with Osip. They spoke in the darkness; to work was a sin, and no one
lighted the lamp. News was exchanged, chiefly disagreeable. Three
houses away the hens had been taken in payment of arrears and sent to
the cantonal office, and there they died of starvation; sheep had also
been taken, and while they were being driven away tied with ropes and
transferred to fresh carts at each village one had died. And now they
discussed the question, Who was responsible?

"The Zemstvo!" said Osip. "Who else?"

"Of course, the Zemstvo!"

They accused the Zemstvo of everything—of arrears, of oppression,
of famines, although not one of them knew exactly what the Zemstvo
was. And that rule had been observed since wealthy peasants with
factories, shops, and houses were elected as Zemstvo members, and
being discontented with the institution, thenceforth in their factories
and inns abused the Zemstvo.

They complained of the fact that God had sent no snow, and that though it was time to lay in firewood, you could neither drive nor walk upon the frozen roads. Fifteen years before, and earlier, the small-talk of Zhukovo was infinitely more entertaining. In those days every old man pretended he held some secret, knew something, and waited for something; they talked of rescripts with gold seals, redistribution of lands, and hidden treasures, and hinted of things mysterious; to-day the people of Zhukovo had no secrets; their life was open to all; and they had no themes for conversation save need, and forage, and the absence of snow. . . .

For a moment they were silent. But soon they remembered the hens and dead sheep, and returned to the problem, Who was responsible?

"The Zemstvo!" said Osip gloomily. "Who else?"

CHAPTER VIII

Died

THE PARISH CHURCH was Kosogorovo, six versts away, but the peasants went there only to christen, marry, or bury; they worshipped at the church across the river. On Sundays, when the weather was fine, the village girls dressed in their best and went in a crowd to the service; and the red, yellow, and green dresses fluttering across the meadow were pleasant to see. In bad weather all stayed at home. They fasted, prayed, and prepared for the sacrament. From those who had failed in this duty during the Great Fast, the priest, when he went round the huts with his crucifix, took fifteen kopecks fine.

The old man did not believe in God, because he had hardly ever thought of Him; he admitted the supernatural, but held that that was an affair for women; and when others spoke of religion, or of miracles, and asked him questions on the subject, he scratched himself and said reluctantly—

"Who knows anything about it?"

Grandmother believed vaguely; in her mind all things were confused, and when she began to meditate on death and salvation, hunger and poverty took the upper hand, and she forgot her meditations. She remembered no prayers, but at night before lying down she stood before the ikons and muttered—

"Mother of God of Kazan, Mother of God of Smolensk, Three-Handed Mother of God. . . ."

Marya and Fekla crossed themselves and fasted, but knew nothing of religion. They neither taught their children to pray nor spoke to them of God; and they taught them no principles save that they must not eat meat during fasts. With the other villagers it was the same; few believed and few understood. Nevertheless, all loved the Scriptures, loved them dearly and piously; the misfortune was that there were no books and no one to read and explain, so that when Olga read aloud the Gospel she was treated with respect, and all addressed her and her daughter Sasha as "You."*

At Church festivals Olga often walked to neighbouring villages, and even to the district town, where there were two monasteries and twenty-seven churches. She was abstracted, and as she walked on her pilgrimage forgot her family. When she returned home it seemed that she had only just discovered her husband and daughter, and she smiled and said radiantly—

"God has sent us His mercy!"

Everything that happened in the village repelled and tormented her. On Elijah's Day they drank, at Assumption they drank, at Elevation they drank. At Intercession Zhukovo had its parish festival; and this the muzhiks observed by drinking for three days; they drank fifty roubles from the communal funds: and then went round the huts and collected money for more vodka. On the first days the Tchikildeyeffs killed a ram, and ate mutton in the morning, at dinner, and for supper; and in the night all the children got out of bed to eat more. Kiriak was drunk all three days; he drank away his cap and boots, and beat Marya so badly that she had to be soused with water. And then all were sick with shame.

Despite this, even this Zhukovo, this Kholuefka, had once a real religious festival. That was in August, when through every village in the district was borne the Life-giving Ikon. The day it was due at Zhukovo was windless and dull. Early in the morning the village girls, in their bright, holiday dress, set out to meet the ikon, which arrived at evening with a procession and singing; and at that moment the church bells rang loudly. A vast crowd from Zhukovo and neighbouring villages filled the street; there were noise, dust, and crushing. And the old man, grandmother, and Kiriak—all stretched out their hands to the ikon, looked at it greedily, and cried with tears—

"Intercessor, Mother! Intercessor!"

All at once, it seemed, realised that there is no void between earth and heaven, that the great and strong of this world have not seized upon everything, that there is intercession against injury, against slavish

*[That is, the polite form of "you," *vy* rather than *ty*.]

subjection, against heavy, intolerable need, against the terrible vodka.
"Intercessor, Mother!" sobbed Marya. "Mother!"

When the service was said and the ikon carried away, all things were
as of old, and noisy, drunken voices echoed from the inn.

Death was dreaded only by the wealthy muzhiks; the richer they
grew the less their faith in God and in salvation; and only out of fear of
the end of the world, to make certain, so to speak, they lighted candles
in the church and said mass. The poorer muzhiks knew no fear of death.
They told the old man and grandmother to their faces that they had
lived their day, that it was high time to die, and the old man and
grandmother listened indifferently. They did not scruple to tell Fekla in
Nikolai's presence that when he, Nikolai, died, her husband, Denis,
would get his discharge from the army and be sent home. And Marya
not only had no fear of death, but was even sorry that it lingered; and
she rejoiced when her own children died.

But though they knew no dread of death, they looked on sickness
with exaggerated dread. The most trifling ailment, a disordered
stomach, a slight chill, sent grandmother on to the stove, where she
rolled herself up, and groaned loudly without cease, "I'm dying!" And
the old man would send for the priest to confess her and administer the
last sacrament. They talked eternally of colds, of worms, of tumours
which begin in the stomach and slowly creep towards the heart. Most of
all they dreaded colds, and even in summer dressed warmly, and
cowered over the stove. Grandmother loved medical treatment, and
constantly drove to hospital, where she said she was fifty-eight instead
of seventy, for she feared that if the doctor knew her age, he would
refuse to treat her, and would tell her it was time to die. She usually
started for the hospital at early morning, taking a couple of the little
girls, and returned at night, hungry and ill-tempered, with a mixture for
herself and ointments for the girls. Once she took with her Nikolai, who
for the next two weeks dosed himself with a mixture and said that he
felt better.

Grandmother knew every doctor, *feldscher,** and wise-woman within
thirty versts and disapproved of all. At Intercession, when the priest
made his round of the huts with a crucifix, the clerk told her that near
the town prison there was an old man, formerly an army *feldscher*, who
doctored cleverly, and he advised grandmother to see him. She took the
advice. When the first snow fell she drove into town, and brought back
an old, bearded Jew in a long caftan, whose whole face was covered with
blue veins. At that time journeymen worked in the hut: an old tailor in

---

*[Doctor's assistant.]

terrifying spectacles made a waistcoat out of rags; and two young lads made felt for top-boots. Kiriak, dismissed for drunkenness, and now living at home, sat beside the tailor and mended a horse-collar. The hut was close and smoky. The Jew looked at Nikolai, and said that he must be bled.

He applied leeches, and the old tailor, Kiriak, and the little girls looked on, and imagined they saw the disease coming out of Nikolai. And Nikolai also watched the leeches sucking his chest, and saw them fill with dark blood; and feeling that, indeed, something was coming out of him, he smiled contentedly.

"It's a good way!" said the tailor. "God grant that it does him good!"

The Jew applied twelve leeches to Nikolai, then twelve more; drank tea, and drove away. Nikolai began to tremble; his face turned haggard, and—as the women put it—dwindled into a fist; his fingers turned blue. He wrapped himself up in the counterpane and then in a sheepskin coat; but felt colder and colder. Towards evening he was peevish; asked them to lay him on the floor, asked the tailor not to smoke, then lay still under the sheepskin; and towards morning died.

CHAPTER IX

Give Alms!

IT WAS a rough, a long winter.

Since Christmas there had been no grain, and flour was bought outside. Kiriak, who still lived at home, made scenes at night, causing terror to all; and next morning his head ached, and he was ashamed, so that it was painful to see him. Night and day in the stall a hungry cow lowed, and rent the hearts of grandmother and Marya. And to make things worse the frost grew severer, and the snow heaped itself high in the street, and the winter stretched out. Annunciation was marked by a genuine winter snowstorm, and snow fell in Holy Week.

But even this ended. The beginning of April brought warm days and frosty nights. Winter gave way reluctantly, but the hot sunshine foiled him, and at last the brooks melted and the birds began to sing. The fields and shrubs by the river-side were hidden in spring floods, and from Zhukovo to the village beyond stretched a big lake, given over to wild duck. The spring sunsets, fiery and with splendid clouds, yielded each day sights new and incredible, sights which are often laughed at when they appear on canvas.

The cranes cried mournfully, as if they called on men to follow them.

Standing on the brink of the ravine, Olga looked at the flood, at the sun, at the bright, it seemed rejuvenated, church; and her tears flowed and she panted with passionate longing to go away, though it might be to the end of the earth. And indeed, it was decided that she should return to Moscow and seek a place as housemaid; and with her would go Kiriak to earn his living as dvornik,* or somehow else. *Akh,* to get away soon!

When the roads dried and the weather turned hot they prepared for the journey. Olga and Sasha with wallets on their backs, both in bast-shoes, left at dawn; and Marya came to see them off. Kiriak, ill, remained for a week more. For the last time Olga prayed towards the church, and thought of her husband, and though she did not cry, her face wrinkled, and seemed ugly, as an old woman's. During the winter she had grown thinner, uglier, and a little grey; instead of the old charm and pleasant smile her face expressed submissiveness and sorrow outlived; and her look was dull and fixed as if she were deaf. She was sorry to leave the village and the muzhiks. She remembered how they carried away Nikolai; how mass was said at nearly every hut; and how all wept, feeling her grief their own. Summer and winter there were hours and days when it seemed to her that these men lived worse than beasts, and to look at them was terrible: they were coarse, dishonest, dirty, drunken; they lived in discord; they fought eternally, because they despised, feared, and suspected one another. Who kept the drink shop and dosed the muzhik with drink? The muzhik. Who squandered and spent on drink the money of the commune, of the school, of the Church? The muzhik. Who stole from his neighbour, burnt his house, perjured himself in court for a bottle of vodka? The muzhik. Who first spoke at the Zemstvo and on other boards against the muzhik? The muzhik. Yes; to live with them was torture! But despite all this, they were men, they suffered and wept as men; and in their whole lives there was not one act for which an excuse might not be found. Labour unbearable, from which the whole body ached at night, fierce winters, scanty harvests, crowding; help from nowhere, and no hope of help! The richer and the stronger gave no help because they themselves were rude, dishonest, intemperate, and foul-tongued; the pettiest official or clerk treated the muzhiks as vagabonds; even the cantonal chiefs and Church elders addressed them as "Thou," and believed they had a right thereto. Yes! And could there be help or good example from the selfish, the greedy, the dissolute, the idle, who came to these villages with but one intent: to insult, terrify, and rob? Olga remembered the piteous, humiliated faces of the old men when in winter Kiriak was brought out

*[House porter, concierge.]

to be flogged! And now she was sorry for all these men and women; and on her last walk through the village she looked at every hut.

When she had accompanied them three versts Marya said good-bye; then fell upon her knees, and with her face touching the ground, cried loudly—

"Again I am left alone; alas, poor me, poor, poor, unfortunate! . . ."

And she continued to keen, so that long afterwards Olga and Sasha could see her on her knees, bent on one side, holding her head with her hands. And above her head flew rocks.

The sun rose higher: the day grew warm. Zhukovo was left far behind. The travellers followed many circuitous paths, and Olga and Sasha soon forgot the village and Marya. They were in good humour, and everything amused them. First a mound; then a line of telegraph posts, with mysterious humming wires, which vanished on the horizon, and sped to some unknown destination; then a farm, buried in green, which sent from afar a smell of dampness and hemp, and seemed to say that it was the home of happy people; then a horse's skeleton lying white in a field. And larks sang untiredly; quails cried to one another; and the landrail cried with a sound like the drawing of an old bolt.

At midday Olga and Sasha reached a big village, and, in the broad street, came upon General Zhukoff's old cook. He was hot, and his red, sweating bald patch shone in the sun. At first he did not recognise Olga; then he looked and recognised her, but both, without exchanging a word, continued their paths. Olga stopped and bowed low before the open windows of a hut which seemed richer and newer than its neighbours, and cried in a loud, thin, and singing voice—

"Orthodox Christians, give alms for the love of Christ; Kingdom of Heaven to your father and mother, eternal rest."

"Orthodox Christians," echoed little Sasha. "Give for the love of Christ, Heavenly Kingdom. . . ."

Gooseberries

FROM EARLY MORNING the sky had been overcast with clouds; the day was still, cool, and wearisome, as usual on grey, dull days when the clouds hang low over the fields and it looks like rain, which never comes. Ivan Ivanich, the veterinary surgeon, and Bourkin, the schoolmaster, were tired of walking and the fields seemed endless to them. Far ahead they could just see the windmills of the village of Mirousky; to the right stretched away, to disappear behind the village, a line of hills, and they knew that it was the bank of the river; meadows, green willows, farmhouses; and from one of the hills there could be seen a field as endless, telegraph posts, and the train, looking from a distance like a crawling caterpillar, and in clear weather even the town. In the calm weather when all Nature seemed gentle and melancholy, Ivan Ivanich and Bourkin were filled with love for the fields and thought how grand and beautiful the country was.

"Last time, when we stopped in Prokufyi's shed," said Bourkin, "you were going to tell me a story."

"Yes. I wanted to tell you about my brother."

Ivan Ivanich took a deep breath and lighted his pipe before beginning his story, but just then the rain began to fall. And in about five minutes it came pelting down and showed no signs of stopping. Ivan Ivanich stopped and hesitated; the dogs, wet through, stood with their tails between their legs and looked at them mournfully.

"We ought to take shelter," said Bourkin. "Let us go to Aliokhin. It is close by."

"Very well."

They took a short cut over a stubble-field and then bore to the right, until they came to the road. Soon there appeared poplars, a garden, the red roofs of granaries; the river began to glimmer and they came to a wide road with a mill and a white bathing-shed. It was Sophino, where Aliokhin lived.

The mill was working, drowning the sound of the rain, and the dam shook. Round the carts stood wet horses, hanging their heads, and men were walking about with their heads covered with sacks. It was wet, muddy, and unpleasant, and the river looked cold and sullen. Ivan Ivanich and Bourkin felt wet and uncomfortable through and through; their feet were tired with walking in the mud, and they walked past the dam to the barn in silence as though they were angry with each other.

In one of the barns a winnowing-machine was working, sending out clouds of dust. On the threshold stood Aliokhin himself, a man of about forty, tall and stout, with long hair, more like a professor or a painter than a farmer. He was wearing a grimy white shirt and rope belt, and pants instead of trousers; and his boots were covered with mud and straw. His nose and eyes were black with dust. He recognised Ivan Ivanich and was apparently very pleased.

"Please, gentlemen," he said, "go to the house. I'll be with you in a minute."

The house was large and two-storied. Aliokhin lived down-stairs in two vaulted rooms with little windows designed for the farm-hands; the farmhouse was plain, and the place smelled of rye bread and vodka, and leather. He rarely used the reception-rooms, only when guests arrived. Ivan Ivanich and Bourkin were received by a chambermaid; such a pretty young woman that both of them stopped and exchanged glances.

"You cannot imagine how glad I am to see you, gentlemen," said Aliokhin, coming after them into the hall. "I never expected you. Pelagueya," he said to the maid, "give my friends a change of clothes. And I will change, too. But I must have a bath. I haven't had one since the spring. Wouldn't you like to come to the bathing-shed? And meanwhile our things will be got ready."

Pretty Pelagueya, dainty and sweet, brought towels and soap, and Aliokhin led his guests to the bathing-shed.

"Yes," he said, "it is a long time since I had a bath. My bathing-shed is all right, as you see. My father and I put it up, but somehow I have no time to bathe."

He sat down on the step and lathered his long hair and neck, and the water round him became brown.

"Yes. I see," said Ivan Ivanich heavily, looking at his head.

"It is a long time since I bathed," said Aliokhin shyly, as he soaped himself again, and the water round him became dark blue, like ink.

Ivan Ivanich came out of the shed, plunged into the water with a splash, and swam about in the rain, flapping his arms, and sending waves back, and on the waves tossed white lilies; he swam out to the middle of the pool and dived, and in a minute came up again in another place and kept on swimming and diving, trying to reach the bottom. "Ah! how delicious!" he shouted in his glee. "How delicious!" He swam to the mill, spoke to the peasants, and came back, and in the middle of the pool he lay on his back to let the rain fall on his face. Bourkin and Aliokhin were already dressed and ready to go, but he kept on swimming and diving.

"Delicious," he said. "Too delicious!"

"You've had enough," shouted Bourkin.

They went to the house. And only when the lamp was lit in the large drawing-room up-stairs, and Bourkin and Ivan Ivanich, dressed in silk dressing-gowns and warm slippers, lounged in chairs, and Aliokhin himself, washed and brushed, in a new frock coat, paced up and down evidently delighting in the warmth and cleanliness and dry clothes and slippers, and pretty Pelagueya, noiselessly tripping over the carpet and smiling sweetly, brought in tea and jam on a tray, only then did Ivan Ivanich begin his story, and it was as though he was being listened to not only by Bourkin and Aliokhin, but also by the old and young ladies and the officer who looked down so staidly and tranquilly from the golden frames.

"We are two brothers," he began, "I, Ivan Ivanich, and Nicholai Ivanich, two years younger. I went in for study and became a veterinary surgeon, while Nicholai was at the Exchequer Court when he was nineteen. Our father, Tchimsha-Himalaysky, was a cantonist, but he died with an officer's rank and left us his title of nobility and a small estate. After his death the estate went to pay his debts. However, we spent our childhood there in the country. We were just like peasants' children, spent days and nights in the fields and the woods, minded the house, barked the lime-trees, fished, and so on. . . . And you know once a man has fished, or watched the thrushes hovering in flocks over the village in the bright, cool, autumn days, he can never really be a townsman, and to the day of his death he will be drawn to the country. My brother pined away in the Exchequer. Years passed and he sat in the same place, wrote out the same documents, and thought of one thing, how to get back to the country. And little by little his distress became a definite disorder, a fixed idea—to buy a small farm somewhere by the bank of a river or a lake.

"He was a good fellow and I loved him, but I never sympathised with the desire to shut oneself up on one's own farm. It is a common saying that a man needs only six feet of land. But surely a corpse wants that, not a man. And I hear that our intellectuals have a longing for the land and want to acquire farms. But it all comes down to the six feet of land. To leave town, and the struggle and the swim of life, and go and hide yourself in a farmhouse is not life—it is egoism, laziness; it is a kind of monasticism, but monasticism without action. A man needs, not six feet of land, not a farm, but the whole earth, all Nature, where in full liberty he can display all the properties and qualities of the free spirit.

"My brother Nicholai, sitting in his office, would dream of eating his own *schi*,* with its savoury smell floating across the farmyard; and of eating out in the open air, and of sleeping in the sun, and of sitting for hours together on a seat by the gate and gazing at the fields and the forest. Books on agriculture and the hints in almanacs were his joy, his favourite spiritual food; and he liked reading newspapers, but only the advertisements of land to be sold, so many acres of arable and grass land, with a farmhouse, river, garden, mill, and mill-pond. And he would dream of garden-walls, flowers, fruits, nests, carp in the pond, don't you know, and all the rest of it. These fantasies of his used to vary according to the advertisements he found, but somehow there was always a gooseberry-bush in every one. Not a house, not a romantic spot could he imagine without its gooseberry-bush.

"'Country life has its advantages,' he used to say. 'You sit on the veranda drinking tea and your ducklings swim on the pond, and everything smells good . . . and there are gooseberries.'

"He used to draw out a plan of his estate and always the same things were shewn on it: (*a*) Farmhouse, (*b*) cottage, (*c*) vegetable garden, (*d*) gooseberry-bush. He used to live meagrely and never had enough to eat and drink, dressed God knows how, exactly like a beggar, and always saved and put his money into the bank. He was terribly stingy. It used to hurt me to see him, and I used to give him money to go away for a holiday, but he would put that away, too. Once a man gets a fixed idea, there's nothing to be done.

"Years passed; he was transferred to another province. He completed his fortieth year and was still reading advertisements in the papers and saving up his money. Then I heard he was married. Still with the same idea of buying a farmhouse with a gooseberry-bush, he married an elderly, ugly widow, not out of any feeling for her, but because she had money. With her he still lived stingily, kept her half-starved, and put the money into the bank in his own name. She had been the wife of a postmaster and was used to good living, but with her second husband she did not even have enough black bread; she pined away in her new life, and in three years or so gave up her soul to God. And my brother never for a moment thought himself to blame for her death. Money, like vodka, can play queer tricks with a man. Once in our town a merchant lay dying. Before his death he asked for some honey, and he ate all his notes and scrip with the honey so that nobody should

*[See page 60.]

get it. Once I was examining a herd of cattle at a station and a horse-jobber fell under the engine, and his foot was cut off. We carried him into the waiting-room, with the blood pouring down—a terrible business—and all the while he kept on asking anxiously for his foot; he had twenty-five roubles in his boot and did not want to lose them."

"Keep to your story," said Bourkin.

"After the death of his wife," Ivan Ivanich continued, after a long pause, "my brother began to look out for an estate. Of course you may search for five years, and even then buy a pig in a poke. Through an agent my brother Nicholai raised a mortgage and bought three hundred acres with a farmhouse, a cottage, and a park, but there was no orchard, no gooseberry-bush, no duck-pond; there was a river but the water in it was coffee-coloured because the estate lay between a brick-yard and a gelatine factory. But my brother Nicholai was not worried about that; he ordered twenty gooseberry-bushes and settled down to a country life.

"Last year I paid him a visit. I thought I'd go and see how things were with him. In his letters my brother called his estate Tchimbarshov Corner, or Himalayskoe. I arrived at Himalayskoe in the afternoon. It was hot. There were ditches, fences, hedges, rows of young fir-trees, trees everywhere, and there was no telling how to cross the yard or where to put your horse. I went to the house and was met by a red-haired dog, as fat as a pig. He tried to bark but felt too lazy. Out of the kitchen came the cook, barefooted, and also as fat as a pig, and said that the master was having his afternoon rest. I went in to my brother and found him sitting on his bed with his knees covered with a blanket; he looked old, stout, flabby; his cheeks, nose, and lips were pendulous. I half expected him to grunt like a pig.

"We embraced and shed a tear of joy and also of sadness to think that we had once been young, but were now both going grey and nearing death. He dressed and took me to see his estate.

"'Well? How are you getting on?' I asked.

"'All right, thank God. I am doing very well.'

"He was no longer the poor, tired official, but a real landowner and a person of consequence. He had got used to the place and liked it, ate a great deal, took Russian baths, was growing fat, had already gone to law with the parish and the two factories, and was much offended if the peasants did not call him 'Your Lordship.' And, like a good landowner, he looked after his soul and did good works pompously, never simply. What good works? He cured the peasants of all kinds of diseases with soda and castor-oil, and on his birthday he would have a thanksgiving service held in the middle of the village, and would treat the peasants to half a bucket of vodka, which he thought the right thing to do. Ah! Those horrible buckets of vodka. One day a greasy landowner will drag the peasants before the Zemstvo* Court for trespass, and the next, if it's a holiday, he will give them a bucket of vodka, and they drink and shout Hooray! and lick his boots in their drunkenness. A change to good eating and idleness always fills a Russian with the most preposterous self-conceit. Nicholai Ivanich, who, when he was in the Exchequer, was terrified to have an opinion of his own, now imagined that what he said was law. 'Education is necessary for the masses, but they are not fit for it.' 'Corporal punishment is generally harmful, but in certain cases it is useful and indispensable.'

"'I know the people and I know how to treat them,' he would say. 'The people love me. I have only to raise my finger and they will do as I wish.'

"And all this, mark you, was said with a kindly smile of wisdom. He was constantly saying: 'We noblemen,' or 'I, as a nobleman.' Apparently he had forgotten that our grandfather was a peasant and our father a common soldier. Even our family name, Tchimsha-Himalaysky, which is really an absurd one, seemed to him full-sounding, distinguished, and very pleasing.

"But my point does not concern him so much as myself. I want to tell you what a change took place in me in those few hours while I was in his house. In the evening, while we were having tea, the cook laid a plateful of gooseberries on the table. They had not been bought, but were his own gooseberries, plucked for the first time since the bushes were planted. Nicholai Ivanich laughed with joy and for a minute or two he looked in silence at the gooseberries with tears in his eyes. He could not speak for excitement, then put one into his mouth, glanced at me in triumph, like a child at last being given its favourite toy, and said:

"'How good they are!'

"He went on eating greedily, and saying all the while:

"'How good they are! Do try one!'

"It was hard and sour, but, as Poushkin said, the illusion which exalts us is dearer to us than ten thousand truths. I saw a happy man, one whose dearest dream had come true, who had attained his goal in life, who had got what he wanted, and was pleased with his destiny and with himself. In my idea of human life there is always some alloy of sadness, but now at the sight of a happy man I was filled with something like despair. And at night it grew on me. A bed was made up for me in the room near my brother's and I could hear him, unable to sleep, going

*[See page 31.]

again and again to the plate of gooseberries. I thought: 'After all, what a lot of contented, happy people there must be! What an overwhelming power that means! I look at this life and see the arrogance and the idleness of the strong, the ignorance and bestiality of the weak, the horrible poverty everywhere, overcrowding, drunkenness, hypocrisy, falsehood . . . Meanwhile in all the houses, all the streets, there is peace; out of fifty thousand people who live in our town there is not one to kick against it all. Think of the people who go to the market for food: during the day they eat; at night they sleep, talk nonsense, marry, grow old, piously follow their dead to the cemetery; one never sees or hears those who suffer, and all the horror of life goes on somewhere behind the scenes. Everything is quiet, peaceful, and against it all there is only the silent protest of statistics; so many go mad, so many gallons are drunk, so many children die of starvation . . . And such a state of things is obviously what we want; apparently a happy man only feels so because the unhappy bear their burden in silence, but for which happiness would be impossible. It is a general hypnosis. Every happy man should have some one with a little hammer at his door to knock and remind him that there are unhappy people, and that, however happy he may be, life will sooner or later show its claws, and some misfortune will befall him—illness, poverty, loss, and then no one will see or hear him, just as he now neither sees nor hears others. But there is no man with a hammer, and the happy go on living, just a little fluttered with the petty cares of every day, like an aspen-tree in the wind—and everything is all right.'

"That night I was able to understand how I, too, had been content and happy," Ivan Ivanich went on, getting up. "I, too, at meals or out hunting, used to lay down the law about living, and religion, and governing the masses. I, too, used to say that teaching is light, that education is necessary, but that for simple folk reading and writing is enough for the present. Freedom is a boon, I used to say, as essential as the air we breathe, but we must wait. Yes—I used to say so, but now I ask: 'Why do we wait?'" Ivan Ivanich glanced angrily at Bourkin. "Why do we wait, I ask you? What considerations keep us fast? I am told that we cannot have everything at once, and that every idea is realised in time. But who says so? Where is the proof that it is so? You refer me to the natural order of things, to the law of cause and effect, but is there order or natural law in that I, a living, thinking creature, should stand by a ditch until it fills up, or is narrowed, when I could jump it or throw a bridge over it? Tell me, I say, why should we wait? Wait, when we have no strength to live, and yet must live and are full of the desire to live!

"I left my brother early the next morning, and from that time on I found it impossible to live in town. The peace and the quiet of it oppress me. I dare not look in at the windows, for nothing is more dreadful to see than the sight of a happy family, sitting round a table, having tea. I am an old man now and am no good for the struggle. I commenced late. I can only grieve within my soul, and fret and sulk. At night my head buzzes with the rush of my thoughts and I cannot sleep . . . Ah! If I were young!"

Ivan Ivanich walked excitedly up and down the room and repeated: "If I were young."

He suddenly walked up to Aliokhin and shook him first by one hand and then by the other.

"Pavel Konstantinich," he said in a voice of entreaty, "don't be satisfied, don't let yourself be lulled to sleep! While you are young, strong, wealthy, do not cease to do good! Happiness does not exist, nor should it, and if there is any meaning or purpose in life, they are not in our piddling little happiness, but in something reasonable and grand. Do good!"

Ivan Ivanich said this with a piteous supplicating smile, as though he were asking a personal favour.

Then they all three sat in different corners of the drawing-room and were silent. Ivan Ivanich's story had satisfied neither Bourkin nor Aliokhin. With the generals and ladies looking down from their gilt frames, seeming alive in the firelight, it was tedious to hear the story of a miserable official who ate gooseberries . . . Somehow they had a longing to hear and to speak of charming people, and of women. And the mere fact of sitting in the drawing-room where everything—the lamp with its coloured shade, the chairs, and the carpet under their feet—told how the very people who now looked down at them from their frames once walked, and sat and had tea there, and the fact that pretty Pelagueya was near—was much better than any story.

Aliokhin wanted very much to go to bed; he had to get up for his work very early, about two in the morning, and now his eyes were closing, but he was afraid of his guests saying something interesting without his hearing it, so he would not go. He did not trouble to think whether what Ivan Ivanich had been saying was clever or right; his guests were talking of neither groats, nor hay, nor tar, but of something which had no bearing on his life, and he liked it and wanted them to go on. . . .

"However, it's time to go to bed," said Bourkin, getting up. "I will wish you good night."

Aliokhin said good night and went down-stairs, and left his guests. Each had a large room with an old wooden bed and carved ornaments;

in the corner was an ivory crucifix; and their wide, cool beds, made by
pretty Pelagueya, smelled sweetly of clean linen.

Ivan Ivanich undressed in silence and lay down.

"God forgive me, a wicked sinner," he murmured, as he drew the
clothes over his head.

A smell of burning tobacco came from his pipe which lay on the table,
and Bourkin could not sleep for a long time and was worried because he
could not make out where the unpleasant smell came from.

The rain beat against the windows all night long.

The Lady with the Toy Dog

IT WAS REPORTED that a new face had been seen on the quay; a lady with a little dog. Dimitri Dimitrich Gomov, who had been a fortnight at Yalta and had got used to it, had begun to show an interest in new faces. As he sat in the pavilion at Verné's he saw a young lady, blond and fairly tall, and wearing a broad-brimmed hat, pass along the quay. After her ran a white Pomeranian.

Later he saw her in the park and in the square several times a day. She walked by herself, always in the same broad-brimmed hat, and with this white dog. Nobody knew who she was, and she was spoken of as the lady with the toy dog.

"If," thought Gomov, "if she is here without a husband or a friend, it would be as well to make her acquaintance."

He was not yet forty, but he had a daughter of twelve and two boys at school. He had married young, in his second year at the University, and now his wife seemed half as old again as himself. She was a tall woman, with dark eyebrows, erect, grave, stolid, and she thought herself an intellectual woman. She read a great deal, called her husband not Dimitri, but Demitri, and in his private mind he thought her short-witted, narrow-minded, and ungracious. He was afraid of her and disliked being at home. He had begun to betray her with other women long ago, betrayed her frequently, and probably for that reason nearly always spoke ill of women, and when they were discussed in his presence he would maintain that they were an inferior race.

It seemed to him that his experience was bitter enough to give him the right to call them any name he liked, but he could not live a couple of days without the "inferior race." With men he was bored and ill at ease, cold and unable to talk, but when he was with women, he felt easy and knew what to talk about, and how to behave, and even when he was silent with them he felt quite comfortable. In his appearance as in his character, indeed in his whole nature, there was something attractive, indefinable, which drew women to him and charmed them; he knew it, and he, too, was drawn by some mysterious power to them.

His frequent, and, indeed, bitter experiences had taught him long ago that every affair of that kind, at first a divine diversion, a delicious smooth adventure, is in the end a source of worry for a decent man, especially for men like those at Moscow who are slow to move, irresolute, domesticated, for it becomes at last an acute and extraordinarily complicated problem and a nuisance. But whenever he met and was interested in a new woman, then his experience would slip away from his memory, and he would long to live, and everything would seem so simple and amusing.

And it so happened that one evening he dined in the gardens, and the lady in the broad-brimmed hat came up at a leisurely pace and sat at the next table. Her expression, her gait, her dress, her coiffure told him that she belonged to society, that she was married, that she was paying her first visit to Yalta, that she was alone, and that she was bored. . . . There is a great deal of untruth in the gossip about the immorality of the place. He scorned such tales, knowing that they were for the most part concocted by people who would be only too ready to sin if they had the chance, but when the lady sat down at the next table, only a yard or two away from him, his thoughts were filled with tales of easy conquests, of trips to the mountains; and he was suddenly possessed by the alluring idea of a quick transitory liaison, a moment's affair with an unknown woman whom he knew not even by name.

He beckoned to the little dog, and when it came up to him, wagged his finger at it. The dog began to growl. Gomov again wagged his finger.

The lady glanced at him and at once cast her eyes down.

"He won't bite," she said and blushed.

"May I give him a bone?"—and when she nodded emphatically, he asked affably: "Have you been in Yalta long?"

"About five days."

"And I am just dragging through my second week."

They were silent for a while.

"Time goes quickly," she said, "and it is amazingly boring here."

"It is the usual thing to say that it is boring here. People live quite happily in dull holes like Bieliev or Zhidra, but as soon as they come here they say: 'How boring it is! The very dregs of dulness!' One would think they came from Spain."

She smiled. Then both went on eating in silence as though they did not know each other; but after dinner they went off together—and then began an easy, playful conversation as though they were perfectly happy, and it was all one to them where they went or what they talked of. They walked and talked of how the sea was strangely luminous; the water lilac, so soft and warm, and athwart it the moon cast a golden streak. They said how stifling it was after the hot day. Gomov told her how he came from Moscow and was a philologist by education, but in a bank by profession; and how he had once wanted to sing in opera, but gave it up; and how he had two houses in Moscow. . . . And from her he learned that she came from Petersburg, was born there, but married at S. where she had been living for the last two years; that she would stay another month at Yalta, and perhaps her husband would come for her, because, he too, needed a rest. She could not tell him what her husband was—Provincial Administration or Zemstvo* Council—and she seemed to think it funny. And Gomov found out that her name was Anna Sergueyevna.

In his room at night, he thought of her and how they would meet next day. They must do so. As he was going to sleep, it struck him that she could only lately have left school, and had been at her lessons even as his daughter was then; he remembered how bashful and gauche she was when she laughed and talked with a stranger—it must be, he thought, the first time she had been alone, and in such a place with men walking after her and looking at her and talking to her, all with the same secret purpose which she could not but guess. He thought of her slender white neck and her pretty, grey eyes.

"There is something touching about her," he thought as he began to fall asleep.

II

A WEEK passed. It was a blazing day. Indoors it was stifling, and in the streets the dust whirled along. All day long he was plagued with thirst and he came into the pavilion every few minutes and offered Anna Sergueyevna an iced drink or an ice. It was impossibly hot.

In the evening, when the air was fresher, they walked to the jetty to see the steamer come in. There was quite a crowd all gathered to meet somebody, for they carried bouquets. And among them were clearly marked the peculiarities of Yalta: the elderly ladies were youngly dressed and there were many generals.

The sea was rough and the steamer was late, and before it turned into the jetty it had to do a great deal of manœuvring. Anna Sergueyevna looked through her lorgnette at the steamer and the passengers as though she were looking for friends, and when she turned to Gomov, her eyes shone. She talked much and her questions were abrupt, and she forgot what she had said; and then she lost her lorgnette in the crowd.

The well-dressed people went away, the wind dropped, and Gomov

*[See page 31.]

Anton Chekhov

and Anna Sergueyevna stood as though they were waiting for somebody to come from the steamer. Anna Sergueyevna was silent. She smelled her flowers and did not look at Gomov.

"The weather has got pleasanter toward evening," he said. "Where shall we go now? Shall we take a carriage?"

She did not answer.

He fixed his eyes on her and suddenly embraced her and kissed her lips, and he was kindled with the perfume and the moisture of the flowers; at once he started and looked round; had not some one seen?

"Let us go to your ——" he murmured.

And they walked quickly away.

Her room was stifling, and smelled of scents which she had bought at the Japanese shop. Gomov looked at her and thought: "What strange chances there are in life!" From the past there came the memory of earlier good-natured women, gay in their love, grateful to him for their happiness, short though it might be; and of others—like his wife—who loved without sincerity, and talked overmuch and affectedly, hysterically, as though they were protesting that it was not love, nor passion, but something more important; and of the few beautiful cold women, into whose eyes there would flash suddenly a fierce expression, a stubborn desire to take, to snatch from life more than it can give; they were no longer in their first youth, they were capricious, unstable, domineering, imprudent, and when Gomov became cold toward them then their beauty roused him to hatred, and the lace on their lingerie reminded him of the scales of fish.

But here there was the shyness and awkwardness of inexperienced youth, a feeling of constraint; an impression of perplexity and wonder, as though some one had suddenly knocked at the door. Anna Sergueyevna, "the lady with the toy dog," took what had happened somehow seriously, with a particular gravity, as though thinking that this was her downfall and very strange and improper. Her features seemed to sink and wither, and on either side of her face her long hair hung mournfully down; she sat crestfallen and musing, exactly like a woman taken in sin in some old picture.

"It is not right," she said. "You are the first to lose respect for me."

There was a melon on the table. Gomov cut a slice and began to eat it slowly. At least half an hour passed in silence.

Anna Sergueyevna was very touching; she irradiated the purity of a simple, devout, inexperienced woman; the solitary candle on the table hardly lighted her face, but it showed her very wretched.

"Why should I cease to respect you?" asked Gomov. "You don't know what you are saying."

"God forgive me!" she said, and her eyes filled with tears. "It is horrible."

"You seem to want to justify yourself."

"How can I justify myself? I am a wicked, low woman and I despise myself. I have no thought of justifying myself. It is not my husband that I have deceived, but myself. And not only now but for a long time past. My husband may be a good honest man, but he is a lackey. I do not know what work he does, but I do know that he is a lackey in his soul. I was twenty when I married him. I was overcome by curiosity. I longed for something. 'Surely,' I said to myself, 'there is another kind of life.' I longed to live! To live, and to live. . . . Curiosity burned me up. . . . You do not understand it, but I swear by God, I could no longer control myself. Something strange was going on in me. I could not hold myself in. I told my husband that I was ill and came here. . . . And here I have been walking about dizzily, like a lunatic. . . . And now I have become a low, filthy woman whom everybody may despise."

Gomov was already bored; her simple words irritated him with their unexpected and inappropriate repentance; but for the tears in her eyes he might have thought her to be joking or playing a part.

"I do not understand," he said quietly. "What do you want?"

She hid her face in his bosom and pressed close to him.

"Believe, believe me, I implore you," she said. "I love a pure, honest life, and sin is revolting to me. I don't know myself what I am doing. Simple people say: 'The devil entrapped me,' and I can say of myself: 'The Evil One tempted me.'"

"Don't, don't," he murmured.

He looked into her staring, frightened eyes, kissed her, spoke quietly and tenderly, and gradually quieted her and she was happy again, and they both began to laugh.

Later, when they went out, there was not a soul on the quay; the town with its cypresses looked like a city of the dead, but the sea still roared and broke against the shore; a boat swung on the waves; and in it sleepily twinkled the light of a lantern.

They found a cab and drove out to the Oreanda.

"Just now in the hall," said Gomov, "I discovered your name written on the board—von Didenitz. Is your husband a German?"

"No. His grandfather, I believe, was a German, but he himself is an Orthodox Russian."

At Oreanda they sat on a bench, not far from the church, looked down at the sea and were silent. Yalta was hardly visible through the morning mist. The tops of the hills were shrouded in motionless white clouds. The leaves of the trees never stirred, the cicadas trilled, and the

monotonous dull sound of the sea, coming up from below, spoke of the
rest, the eternal sleep awaiting us. So the sea roared when there was
neither Yalta nor Oreanda, and so it roars and will roar, dully,
indifferently when we shall be no more. And in this continual
indifference to the life and death of each of us lives pent up the pledge
of our eternal salvation, of the uninterrupted movement of life on earth
and its unceasing perfection. Sitting side by side with a young woman,
who in the dawn seemed so beautiful, Gomov, appeased and enchanted
by the sight of the fairy scene, the sea, the mountains, the clouds, the
wide sky, thought how at bottom, if it were thoroughly explored,
everything on earth was beautiful, everything, except what we
ourselves think and do when we forget the higher purposes of life and
our own human dignity.

A man came up—a coast-guard—gave a look at them, then went
away. He, too, seemed mysterious and enchanted. A steamer came over
from Feodossia, by the light of the morning star, its own lights already
put out.

"There is dew on the grass," said Anna Sergueyevna after a silence.

"Yes. It is time to go home."

They returned to the town.

Then every afternoon they met on the quay, and lunched together,
dined, walked, enjoyed the sea. She complained that she slept badly,
that her heart beat alarmingly. She would ask the same question over
and over again, and was troubled now by jealousy, now by fear that he
did not sufficiently respect her. And often in the square or the gardens,
when there was no one near, he would draw her close and kiss her
passionately. Their complete idleness, these kisses in the full daylight,
given timidly and fearfully lest any one should see, the heat, the smell
of the sea and the continual brilliant parade of leisured, well-dressed,
well-fed people almost regenerated him. He would tell Anna Sergueyevna how delightful she was, how tempting. He was impatiently
passionate, never left her side, and she would often brood, and even
asked him to confess that he did not respect her, did not love her at all,
and only saw in her a loose woman. Almost every evening, rather late,
they would drive out of the town, to Oreanda, or to the waterfall; and
these drives were always delightful, and the impressions won during
them were always beautiful and sublime.

They expected her husband to come. But he sent a letter in which he
said that his eyes were bad and implored his wife to come home. Anna
Sergueyevna began to worry.

"It is a good thing I am going away," she would say to Gomov. "It is
fate."

She went in a carriage and he accompanied her. They drove for a
whole day. When she took her seat in the car of an express-train and
when the second bell sounded, she said:
"Let me have another look at you. . . . Just one more look. Just as
you are."
She did not cry, but was sad and low-spirited, and her lips trembled.
"I will think of you—often," she said. "Good-bye. Good-bye. Don't
think ill of me. We part for ever. We must, because we ought not to
have met at all. Now, good-bye."
The train moved off rapidly. Its lights disappeared, and in a minute
or two the sound of it was lost, as though everything were agreed to put
an end to this sweet, oblivious madness. Left alone on the platform,
looking into the darkness, Gomov heard the trilling of the grasshoppers
and the humming of the telegraph-wires, and felt as though he had just
woke up. And he thought that it had been one more adventure, one
more affair, and it also was finished and had left only a memory. He was
moved, sad, and filled with a faint remorse; surely the young woman,
whom he would never see again, had not been happy with him; he had
been kind to her, friendly, and sincere, but still in his attitude toward
her, in his tone and caresses, there had always been a thin shadow of
raillery, the rather rough arrogance of the successful male aggravated
by the fact that he was twice as old as she. And all the time she had
called him kind, remarkable, noble, so that he was never really himself
to her, and had involuntarily deceived her. . . .
Here at the station, the smell of autumn was in the air, and the
evening was cool.
"It is time for me to go North," thought Gomov, as he left the
platform. "It is time."

III

AT HOME IN MOSCOW, it was already like winter; the stoves were
heated, and in the mornings, when the children were getting ready to go
to school, and had their tea, it was dark and their nurse lighted the lamp
for a short while. The frost had already begun. When the first snow
falls, the first day of driving in sledges, it is good to see the white earth,
the white roofs; one breathes easily, eagerly, and then one remembers
the days of youth. The old lime-trees and birches, white with hoarfrost,
have a kindly expression; they are nearer to the heart than cypresses
and palm-trees, and with the dear familiar trees there is no need to
think of mountains and the sea.
Gomov was a native of Moscow. He returned to Moscow on a fine
frosty day, and when he donned his fur coat and warm gloves, and took

a stroll through Petrovka, and when on Saturday evening he heard the church-bells ringing, then his recent travels and the places he had visited lost all their charms. Little by little he sank back into Moscow life, read eagerly three newspapers a day, and said that he did not read Moscow papers as a matter of principle. He was drawn into a round of restaurants, clubs, dinner-parties, parties, and he was flattered to have his house frequented by famous lawyers and actors, and to play cards with a professor at the University club. He could eat a whole plateful of hot *sielianka.**

So a month would pass, and Anna Sergueyevna, he thought, would be lost in the mists of memory and only rarely would she visit his dreams with her touching smile, just as other women had done. But more than a month passed, full winter came, and in his memory everything was clear, as though he had parted from Anna Sergueyevna only yesterday. And his memory was lit by a light that grew ever stronger. No matter how, through the voices of his children saying their lessons, penetrating to the evening stillness of his study, through hearing a song, or the music in a restaurant, or the snow-storm howling in the chimney, suddenly the whole thing would come to life again in his memory: the meeting on the jetty, the early morning with the mists on the mountains, the steamer from Feodossia and their kisses. He would pace up and down his room and remember it all and smile, and then his memories would drift into dreams, and the past was confused in his imagination with the future. He did not dream at night of Anna Sergueyevna, but she followed him everywhere, like a shadow, watching him. As he shut his eyes, he could see her, vividly, and she seemed handsomer, tenderer, younger than in reality; and he seemed to himself better than he had been at Yalta. In the evenings she would look at him from the bookcase, from the fireplace, from the corner; he could hear her breathing and the soft rustle of her dress. In the street he would gaze at women's faces to see if there were not one like her. . . .

He was filled with a great longing to share his memories with some one. But at home it was impossible to speak of his love, and away from home—there was no one. Impossible to talk of her to the other people in the house and the men at the bank. And talk of what? Had he loved then? Was there anything fine, romantic, or elevating or even interesting in his relations with Anna Sergueyevna? And he would speak vaguely of love, of women, and nobody guessed what was the matter, and only his wife would raise her dark eyebrows and say:

"Demitri, the rôle of coxcomb does not suit you at all."

*[Thick soup, or steamed cabbage, with meat or fish.]

One night, as he was coming out of the club with his partner, an official, he could not help saying:

"If only I could tell what a fascinating woman I met at Yalta."

The official seated himself in his sledge and drove off, but suddenly called:

"Dimitri Dimitrich!"

"Yes."

"You were right. The sturgeon was tainted."

These banal words suddenly roused Gomov's indignation. They seemed to him degrading and impure. What barbarous customs and people!

What preposterous nights, what dull, empty days! Furious card-playing, gourmandising, drinking, endless conversations about the same things, futile activities and conversations taking up the best part of the day and all the best of man's forces, leaving only a stunted, wingless life, just rubbish; and to go away and escape was impossible—one might as well be in a lunatic asylum or in prison with hard labour.

Gomov did not sleep that night, but lay burning with indignation, and then all next day he had a headache. And the following night he slept badly, sitting up in bed and thinking, or pacing from corner to corner of his room. His children bored him, the bank bored him, and he had no desire to go out or speak to any one.

In December when the holidays came he prepared to go on a journey and told his wife he was going to Petersburg to present a petition for a young friend of his—and went to S. Why? He did not know. He wanted to see Anna Sergueyevna, to talk to her, and if possible to arrange an assignation.

He arrived at S. in the morning and occupied the best room in the hotel, where the whole floor was covered with a grey canvas, and on the table there stood an inkstand grey with dust, adorned with a horseman on a headless horse holding a net in his raised hand. The porter gave him the necessary information: von Didenitz; Old Goncharna Street, his own house—not far from the hotel; lives well, has his own horses, every one knows him.

Gomov walked slowly to Old Goncharna Street and found the house. In front of it was a long, grey fence spiked with nails.

"No getting over a fence like that," thought Gomov, glancing from the windows to the fence.

He thought: "To-day is a holiday and her husband is probably at home. Besides it would be tactless to call and upset her. If he sent a note then it might fall into her husband's hands and spoil everything. It would be better to wait for an opportunity." And he kept on walking up and down the street, and round the fence, waiting for his opportunity. He saw a beggar go in at the gate and the dogs attack him. He heard a piano and the sounds came faintly to his ears. It must be Anna Sergueyevna playing. The door suddenly opened and out of it came an old woman, and after her ran the familiar white Pomeranian. Gomov wanted to call the dog, but his heart suddenly began to thump and in his agitation he could not remember the dog's name.

He walked on, and more and more he hated the grey fence and thought with a gust of irritation that Anna Sergueyevna had already forgotten him, and was perhaps already amusing herself with some one else, as would be only natural in a young woman forced from morning to night to behold the accursed fence. He returned to his room and sat for a long time on the sofa, not knowing what to do. Then he dined and afterward slept for a long while.

"How idiotic and tiresome it all is," he thought as he awoke and saw the dark windows; for it was evening. "I've had sleep enough, and what shall I do to-night?"

He sat on his bed, which was covered with a cheap, grey blanket, exactly like those used in a hospital, and tormented himself.

"So much for the lady with the toy dog. . . . So much for the great adventure. . . . Here you sit."

However, in the morning, at the station, his eye had been caught by a poster with large letters: "First Performance of 'The Geisha.'" He remembered that and went to the theatre.

"It is quite possible she will go to the first performance," he thought.

The theatre was full and, as usual in all provincial theatres, there was a thick mist above the lights, the gallery was noisily restless; in the first row before the opening of the performance stood the local dandies with their hands behind their backs, and there in the governor's box, in front, sat the governor's daughter, and the governor himself sat modestly behind the curtain and only his hands were visible. The curtain quivered; the orchestra tuned up for a long time, and while the audience were coming in and taking their seats, Gomov gazed eagerly round.

At last Anna Sergueyevna came in. She took her seat in the third row, and when Gomov glanced at her his heart ached and he knew that for him there was no one in the whole world nearer, dearer, and more important than she; she was lost in this provincial rabble, the little undistinguished woman, with a common lorgnette in her hands, yet she filled his whole life; she was his grief, his joy, his only happiness, and he longed for her; and through the noise of the bad orchestra with its tenth-rate fiddles, he thought how dear she was to him. He thought and dreamed.

With Anna Sergueyevna there came in a young man with short
side-whiskers, very tall, stooping; with every movement he shook and
bowed continually. Probably he was the husband whom in a bitter
mood at Yalta she had called a lackey. And, indeed, in his long figure,
his side-whiskers, the little bald patch on the top of his head, there was
something of the lackey; he had a modest sugary smile and in his
buttonhole he wore a University badge exactly like a lackey's number.

In the first entr'acte the husband went out to smoke, and she was left
alone. Gomov, who was also in the pit, came up to her and said in a
trembling voice with a forced smile:

"How do you do?"

She looked up at him and went pale. Then she glanced at him again in
terror, not believing her eyes, clasped her fan and lorgnette tightly
together, apparently struggling to keep herself from fainting. Both were
silent. She sat, he stood; frightened by her emotion, not daring to sit
down beside her. The fiddles and flutes began to play and suddenly it
seemed to them as though all the people in the boxes were looking at
them. She got up and walked quickly to the exit; he followed, and both
walked absently along the corridors, down the stairs, up the stairs, with
the crowd shifting and shimmering before their eyes; all kinds of
uniforms, judges, teachers, crown-estates, and all with badges; ladies
shone and shimmered before them, like fur coats on moving rows of
clothes-pegs, and there was a draught howling through the place laden
with the smell of tobacco and cigar-ends. And Gomov, whose heart was
thudding wildly, thought:

"Oh, Lord! Why all these men and that beastly orchestra?"

At that very moment he remembered how when he had seen Anna
Sergueyevna off that evening at the station he had said to himself that
everything was over between them, and they would never meet again.
And now how far off they were from the end!

On a narrow, dark staircase over which was written: "This Way to
the Amphitheatre," she stopped:

"How you frightened me!" she said, breathing heavily, still pale and
apparently stupefied. "Oh! how you frightened me! I am nearly dead.
Why did you come? Why?"

"Understand me, Anna," he whispered quickly. "I implore you to
understand. . . ."

She looked at him fearfully, in entreaty, with love in her eyes, gazing
fixedly to gather up in her memory every one of his features.

"I suffer so!" she went on, not listening to him. "All the time, I
thought only of you. I lived with thoughts of you. . . . And I wanted to
forget, to forget, but why, why did you come?"

A little above them, on the landing, two schoolboys stood and smoked and looked down at them, but Gomov did not care. He drew her to him and began to kiss her cheeks, her hands.

"What are you doing? What are you doing?" she said in terror, thrusting him away. . . . "We were both mad. Go away to-night. You must go away at once. . . . I implore you, by everything you hold sacred, I implore you. . . . The people are coming——"

Some one passed them on the stairs.

"You must go away," Anna Sergueyevna went on in a whisper. "Do you hear, Dimitri Dimitrich? I'll come to you in Moscow. I never was happy. Now I am unhappy and I shall never, never be happy, never! Don't make me suffer even more! I swear, I'll come to Moscow. And now let us part. My dear, dearest darling, let us part!"

She pressed his hand and began to go quickly downstairs, all the while looking back at him, and in her eyes plainly showed that she was most unhappy. Gomov stood for a while, listened, then, when all was quiet he found his coat and left the theatre.

IV

AND ANNA SERGUEYEVNA began to come to him in Moscow. Once every two or three months she would leave S., telling her husband that she was going to consult a specialist in women's diseases. Her husband half believed and half disbelieved her. At Moscow she would stay at the "Slaviansky Bazaar" and send a message at once to Gomov. He would come to her, and nobody in Moscow knew.

Once as he was going to her as usual one winter morning—he had not received her message the night before—he had his daughter with him, for he was taking her to school which was on the way. Great wet flakes of snow were falling.

"Three degrees above freezing," he said, "and still the snow is falling. But the warmth is only on the surface of the earth. In the upper strata of the atmosphere there is quite a different temperature."

"Yes, papa. Why is there no thunder in winter?"

He explained this too, and as he spoke he thought of his assignation, and that not a living soul knew of it, or ever would know. He had two lives; one obvious, which every one could see and know, if they were sufficiently interested, a life full of conventional truth and conventional fraud, exactly like the lives of his friends and acquaintances; and another, which moved underground. And by a strange conspiracy of circumstances, everything that was to him important, interesting, vital, everything that enabled him to be sincere and denied self-deception and was the very core of his being, must dwell hidden away from others, and everything that made him false, a mere shape in which he hid himself in order to conceal the truth, as for instance his work in the bank, arguments at the club, his favourite gibe about women, going to parties with his wife—all this was open. And, judging others by himself, he did not believe the things he saw, and assumed that everybody else also had his real vital life passing under a veil of mystery as under the cover of the night. Every man's intimate existence is kept mysterious, and perhaps, in part, because of that civilised people are so nervously anxious that a personal secret should be respected.

When he had left his daughter at school, Gomov went to the "Slaviansky Bazaar." He took off his fur coat down-stairs, went up and knocked quietly at the door. Anna Sergueyevna, wearing his favourite grey dress, tired by the journey, had been expecting him to come all night. She was pale, and looked at him without a smile, and flung herself on his breast as soon as he entered. Their kiss was long and lingering as though they had not seen each other for a couple of years.

"Well, how are you getting on down there?" he asked. "What is your news?"

"Wait. I'll tell you presently. . . . I cannot."

She could not speak, for she was weeping. She turned her face from him and dried her eyes.

"Well, let her cry a bit . . . . I'll wait," he thought, and sat down.

Then he rang and ordered tea, and then, as he drank it, she stood and gazed out of the window. . . . She was weeping in distress, in the bitter knowledge that their life had fallen out so sadly; only seeing each other in secret, hiding themselves away like thieves! Was not their life crushed?

"Don't cry. . . . Don't cry," he said.

It was clear to him that their love was yet far from its end, which there was no seeing. Anna Sergueyevna was more and more passionately attached to him; she adored him and it was inconceivable that he should tell her that their love must some day end; she would not believe it.

He came up to her and patted her shoulder fondly and at that moment he saw himself in the mirror.

His hair was already going grey. And it seemed strange to him that in the last few years he should have got so old and ugly. Her shoulders were warm and trembled to his touch. He was suddenly filled with pity for her life, still so warm and beautiful, but probably beginning to fade and wither, like his own. Why should she love him so much? He always seemed to women not what he really was, and they loved in him, not himself, but the creature of their imagination, the thing they hankered for in life, and when they had discovered their mistake, still they loved him. And not one of them was happy with him. Time passed; he met women and was friends with them, went further and parted, but never once did he love; there was everything but love.

And now at last when his hair was grey he had fallen in love—real love—for the first time in his life.

Anna Sergueyevna and he loved one another, like dear kindred, like husband and wife, like devoted friends; it seemed to them that Fate had destined them for one another, and it was inconceivable that he should have a wife, she a husband; they were like two birds of passage, a male and a female, which had been caught and forced to live in separate cages. They had forgiven each other all the past of which they were ashamed; they forgave everything in the present, and they felt that their love had changed both of them.

Formerly, when he felt a melancholy compunction, he used to comfort himself with all kinds of arguments, just as they happened to cross his mind, but now he was far removed from any such ideas; he was filled with a profound pity, and he desired to be tender and sincere. . . .

"Don't cry, my darling," he said. "You have cried enough. . . . Now let us talk and see if we can't find some way out."

Then they talked it all over, and tried to discover some means of avoiding the necessity for concealment and deception, and the torment of living in different towns, and of not seeing each other for a long time. How could they shake off these intolerable fetters?

"How? How?" he asked, holding his head in his hands. "How?"

And it seemed that but a little while and the solution would be found and there would begin a lovely new life; and to both of them it was clear that the end was still very far off, and that their hardest and most difficult period was only just beginning.